Ancestral Women's Series:
Book One

The Legend of Randine: Entering the Sisterhood

by

Robin H. Lysne, Ph.D.

Blue Bone Books

Santa Cruz, CA

Publisher's Page

Copyright 2021
Robin H. Lysne, M.F.A., Ph.D.

Blue Bone Books
P.O. Box 2250
Santa Cruz, CA 95063
United States of America

This book is Book One of the Ancestral Women's Series.

ISBN#:

The Legend of Randine: Entering the Sisterhood
978-1-948675 06-2   Book

Library of Congress #:2021913040

The Legend of Randine, Entering the Sisterhood
978-1-948675-07-9   E-book

Table of Contents

This book is dedicated to all
who mother,
whether they have children or not,
and to the Divine Mother
who lives through all of us.

Ancestral Women's Series:
Book One

The Legend of Randine: Entering the Sisterhood

by

Robin H. Lysne, Ph.D.

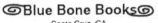
Blue Bone Books
Santa Cruz, CA

Prologue

Discovering Randine

Gudvagen, Norway
Thursday, August 22, 1995
Robin Lysne's Journal
Tomorrow I finally go to Laerdal, after three days in Bergen,
a fairly rainy town. But the people are so kind and helpful...
They make me glad to be Norwegian!

It was time to take the ancestral journey of a lifetime to visit
the places my family had come from on both sides. Only
three months before in May, mom had died of pancreatic
cancer. Shortly after her death, I received a small grant for a
writing project I was working on. It was enough to make the
trip to Norway and visit a few friends in England.

As both my grandfathers were Norwegian, one from
Kragerø near Oslo, the other from Laerdal closer to Bergen,
I started in Oslo the other side of the country from Bergen.
I had already stayed with the only known cousin left on
my father's side in Kragerø, south of Oslo. I had traveled
by train to Oslo, then Lillehammer, and finally Bergen. No
relatives lived in Lillehammer, only friends of a sister and
people who everywhere looked a lot like me.

Finally I arrived in Bergen, my last stop in Norway,
where I was going to visit my mother's family homestead in
Laerdal on her father's side with the name of Lysne. Grandpa Lysne's ghost could be everywhere I turned in Bergen. I
saw men that could be one of his long lost brothers. I was
fortunate to have known all four grandparents until I was

twenty-three, so I knew them all well.

I spent the last three days in Bergen getting my driver's license faxed to the car rental office by my elderly father, as I had forgotten my license when I left the states. Three additional days in Bergen was not part of my plan. Why am I here? I kept asking. The delay would force me to loose time in Laerdal as I had to make it back for a boat trip across the North Sea to Newcastle just one day after I got back to Bergen.

Bergen was a bustling city and the busy seaport. I did get a chance to stop at the University, where I was able to do some research on family history. I took a walk through town and around the harbor, and visited a pond with small boats and swans in it. I watched a loving grandfather show his grandson how to launch a wooden boat with a pole, after he set the sails. I thought, this must be a tradition on this pond with this family.

Just my luck, the harbor got socked in with thick fog and rain and my gondola trip up the local mountain summit was cold and rainy. I could only see cloud banks from the gondola, with mountains sticking through as the wet wind blew down my jacket. At the top I stood on a stone deck, straining to see through the clouds and suddenly, the sun peeked out for a few minutes. The scene was breathtaking. Islands outside the harbor dotted the sea below, waves crashed on rocks everywhere around the islands, and the harbor. I got a feel for Bergen, its weather and rain. There must be a reason for this, I thought.

The man at the car rental agency laughed as he showed me how well my picture turned out on the fax of my driver's license when it finally came through.

"Do you think anyone who stopped me would know it's me?" He chuckled and let me rent the car anyway.

"At least the name is the same as on your passport. Just try not to get stopped." He made a copy so I would have one in my wallet. That photocopy was even worse with two white holes for eyes. You could not make out my facial features at all.

Following the map the rental agent gave me; I drove for over an hour to the dock early the next morning. The road to Gudvagen was like any two lane country road with rocks and mountains around me. The houses were wood framed painted white, though some in the country were red with white trim. The western Norwegian rains had finally stopped once I got to Gudvagen. There was only one ferry a day, so I had to be on time. As I drove into line to board the ferryboat, which left at noon, I could see by the schedule that we would get to Laerdal by sun down. I would be traveling the same route my ancestors took to get to America. This much I knew, but not much else as I watched from the dock as the dot of a boat got bigger and bigger from way down the fjord. Mostly, I had birth dates and death dates of my ancestors and that was about it. There were things written in Norwegian, but mostly descriptions of farms, or so I thought.

This body of water was the Sogn og Fjordaine, the largest finger of water that stretched 150 miles inland to Laerdal, the place of my ancestors on my mother's side. I could hardly take in actually being ready to begin the voyage to Laerdal. I had heard about it from my Grandfather as a child as he had heard stories from his father's father, Grandpa Henrik. But I had never even seen pictures of the fjords until I was standing on the shore of one. The scene made my body tingle with excitement. Jagged mountains rose straight up from water as deep as the mountains were high. Their snow-covered tops appeared as another layer beyond cliffs carved by fjord waters. Waterfalls were pouring randomly out of the rock face hundreds of feet up, trickling down the rocks into small streams.

Gudvagen was so much simpler a port than I had expected. There was no town, not even a group of houses. This finger of fjord ended with rocks lining the water, and a green mowed lawn stretching between the water and the road. On one end, far away from the dock was a red wooden farmhouse with a long shed under some trees that looked like a chicken coop or a barn. On the other side of the grassy field, about 100 meters from the barn, was a dock with a small sign that said, Gudvagen Ferje (Ferry). There was a small ticket shed, about three feet by three feet, with a man who sold tickets. That was it. No ferry building, no ice cream store, nor T-shirt shop, not even a candy shack. In any American tourist place, they would be selling T-shirts and trinkets, not to mention sugar coated candy with the location name emblazoned on everything!

As the Ferry pulled up and emptied its cargo, which consisted of a long line of cars and passengers, I walked over to my car and started my engine. Driving into the hull of the four-story boat, I felt a sense of excitement as the first of my family to return to the place of my ancestors. My parents had taken a quick, whirlwind bus trip through Norway, and came this way on the ferry, but had not spent any amount of time except to pass through the place. I would have two days to explore my ancestral home. It wasn't much time, but it was something. Perhaps I would visit the cemetery and the church to see about family records.

On the boat, my senses took in the boat and the mountains, the pristine air, and the faces of the people. I tried to memorize every moment of this adventure to bring home to my family. I snapped many pictures like the other tourists. Once my car was parked inside the ferry, and I was free to roam around the boat, I found that no one was speaking English. Most of the passengers were German, Norwegian, or from other countries, accents unrecognizable. After getting a cup of coffee with cream, and a cheese sandwich, I sat on the top deck to look at the scenery and to people watch.

Not ten minutes after its initial docking to unload passengers the boat loaded all the cars and people and pulled away full of new passengers. Speaking first in Norwegian and then in English, the captain explained that we were not just a tourist boat, but also the only transport between Bergen and Oslo through the fjord for some people, AND we were also on an official mail boat that would be docking mid-fjord with a smaller boat in about two hours.

Chills of excitement ran up and down my arms, as we made our way to Laerdal. I felt that something important was about to happen. The mountains rose so high you could not see the tops. Every once in a while, a stream made waterfalls jetting out of a sheer rock wall. Sometimes where there had been a landslide that had grown over with vibrant green, there in the grassy slope was a small isolated wooden farmhouse. Often it was nestled among a small apple orchard with a rickety dock jutting out from the hillside. As we glided by steep rock walls, sheep and goats dotted pastures high above the fjord. Only occasionally did I see people in other boats or on the mountainsides. For one thing, it was much too steep, but also, we were in untamed wilderness most of the way.

Every turn around another bend was more breathtaking than the last. I felt my ancestral roots growing right through the boat and diving down into the icy, dark, tannin-stained water. The sides of the mountains plunged down under the boat into the seawater as the passengers and I chugged along in the ferryboat, taking it all in. Rain fell in squalls, on then off, then on again, but since it was August, it did not matter to me. I could only imagine how cold it must get in the winter. I noticed in the brochure that the ferries were only in service from May to September, perhaps too cold and not enough tourism. Most of the ferryboat was enclosed except for an open deck on each level. I found a place where I could sit out of the rain.

It took all afternoon to travel to Laerdal. The exhaust from the smoke stack huffed and puffed and I thought how sad it was that any amount of pollution at all would touch this pristine landscape. I was falling in love with Norway and feeling protective of it's beauty.

As we traveled through the harsh and beautiful fjords, so chill and fresh, I could see how the Norwegian people were inspired to create their gods from the mountains and ice pack. The unrelenting strength of Thor, and beauty and wisdom of Frigg were embedded in the land.

Hours later, as we approached the Laerdal dock, I was surprised once again at how simple a place it was. No Disney commercialism here, no sign announcing anything that was not necessary for tourist's information. I followed the other passengers in their cars off the boat and followed the letter "I" to the tourist bureau. I had learned in Bergen that "I" for "information" was the universal sign used in most of Europe for helping tourists. Laerdal was a small village of a few white wood-frame houses and a hotel that made up the central village. Houses in the valley snaked along the river that rushed down the valley to the fjord. Every building was painted white with black tile roofs. Two churches, down the road rested on either side of the river. One an ancient Stave Church, originally made by Vikings, and the other a small Christian church both with cemeteries.

Inside the tourist bureau, a small cabin-like structure alongside the hotel, was a kind looking woman who was in charge of the tourist bureau.

"Hallo," she said cheerily.

"God Kveld (Good Evening)," I replied in my very bad Norwegian.

"May I help you?" She asked in broken English.

"Yes, my name is Robin Lysne, my ancestors are from Laerdal. Can you tell me where the cemetery is?"

"Ah, Loosna," she said, pronouncing the name in Norwegian. "I thought you looked familiar. Would you like me to call Hoken?"

"Who is Hoken?"

"Your cousin."

"My cousin?!!! I did not know I had any cousins left!"

"Ah, Laerdal is only 2000 souls, everyone knows everyone here. Yes, you have family here and not just in the cemeteries," she said, smiling.

"I wouldn't want to bother them. I–I really did not expect to find my family."

"Ah, so Norwegian! You don't want to bother them," she said smiling broadly.

"Do you know about the Big Book, then?"

"The Big Book?"

"Ya, it is a book of all the farms and government papers gathered in several volumes. It was a labor of love by a dear man who spent twenty-five years collecting all the documents. Here is the section your family is in, here."

The woman brought out a huge book at least three feet high and two feet wide, with a cover that was printed with the name of the area that we were in, Laerdalsori. Each book had district names listed, then the groups of farms and the families. She opened it to the page where I could see my family name at the top, Lysne, or Lysøne, in the ancient script, with a list of family members and names, and pictures of the farms and the people who lived there over time. Of course all the information was written in Norwegian. But I found my great-great grandfather, Henrik, and his parents, Ola and Randine.

"Oh yes, I saw this in Bergen, at the University. They gave me copies of the page," I smiled, "I did not know it had the name "Big Book."

As she read the information, she looked at me out of the corner of her eye, and then suddenly she looked directly at me.

"Do you know about your great, great grandfather?" She asked cautiously.

"Yes, Henrik Lysne, he was my grandfather's grandfather. He came to the U.S. with his wife and children."

"Did you know he was illegitimate?"

Surprised, I laughed nervously, and said, "No, that story never made it across the Atlantic."

"Well, it says here, on his immigration papers, that his mother, was named by Henrik as Randine. Yet here in another document, it says that Randine was trained in Oslo (then called Christiania) as a midwife and was a wet nurse for him, not his real mother."

"So, she was probably the only mother he knew," I said, feeling compassion for him, and trying not to show my irritation at her implication. "That is very interesting."

"Where are you staying?" She asked.

"At the B & B around the corner."

"Ah, yes, well I own the hotel next door. I am Mrs. Larsen, of the Larsen Hotel. So nice to meet you, Miss Lysne."

"Please call me Robin. Thank you for the information. It is getting late. I must get some rest if I am going to explore Laerdal tomorrow. God natt (good night)." I tried again to use some Norwegian with the few words I knew.

When I got to the B & B, I had a message to call Hoken Lysne. Mrs. Larsen had called my cousin, and I was invited to dinner at his home the next day.

After a large Norwegian breakfast at the hotel, I decided that I would switch to the hotel that night. The breakfast spread convinced me, as there were several kinds of herring; pickled, in cream, in onions and wine, and in an assortment of other variations; along with flat bread, dark rye, eggs, and oatmeal; not to mention dried raisins, apricots, bacon, sausage, and smoked salmon, all laid out on a Smorgasbord with long tables. Herring was my favorite in any sauce. So Norwegian, I chuckled to myself.

After breakfast I drove down the road to a sign that said, "Lysøne, and I noticed the archaic spelling that I had never seen before. I few meters past the sign, there was a tall man standing on the porch of a vacant store off to the left of the road. He looked remarkably like my nephew Nathan. The height was unmistakable, as he was over 6'5" and very thin. He could have been Nate's father or brother. He was younger than I was it seemed to me, perhaps by a few years.

"That must be Hoken, no mistaking him!" I said out loud.

It was raining slightly, so I pulled the car over and he folded himself with his umbrella into the passenger seat of my small, compact car. After shaking hands, and greeting me warmly, he directed me up a road to the left off the main road, about 20 meters from where I had picked him up.

The road turned out to be the driveway and was not paved, but full of gravel as we chugged up the hill. We stopped at a sweet house that seemed rather new. It hung on the edge of the hill we had just come up.

"This is our house," he said in very good English. "We have just had a baby, come in and meet my wife."

As he opened the colorful dark teal door, the room was an open floor plan with a kitchen on the right and a view in front of us of the Laerdal Valley. It was so beautiful through the windows I longed to go out to the porch. Instead I greeted his wife Sigrid and his new son.

Their house was simple with little furniture, but all handmade. There was wainscoting around the room, about chest high, painted green with red trim. The house was colorful inside, painted another shade above the wainscoting.

Sigrid could not speak much English, but Hoken was fluent in both languages. Their darling baby boy, Lars Hokanson Lysne, was only a few months old. They were very kind and generous spirits. Sigrid cooked while Hoken and I poured over many family pictures in albums he kept in his office. He gave me a copy of a journal sent to him by a relative I did not know, who lived in the U.S. Another Lysne.

"There aren't that many of us left here," Hoken said, "My brother, who was the first born, lives in the main farmhouse with his family. My parents live up the hill in the next house. My sister lives in town with her family. Perhaps you can meet them later. Bob Lysne, who sent me this album, is from Minnesota. He stayed with us for several weeks one summer."

Midday, after we had eaten, Hoken gave me a tour of the farm and his little plot of land. Hoken showed me grapes he was growing, "from Napa Valley," he said with a smile. "You know Napa?"

"Yes, very well," I said, "I lived in California before my mother got ill."

Later he took me up to his brother's house. It was raining slightly, but I didn't care. After learning his parents were traveling, we met his brother and children at the other farmhouse, the one my great, great, great grandfather, Ola, grew up in, and I realized this was a double historical event. This very house is where generations had lived for as long as anyone could remember. Besides meeting Hoken and his family, I was actually seeing where my ancestors had lived 150 years ago!

Since both Hoken and I were keenly interested in our heritage, after we returned to his house, I gave him a copy of my first book, Dancing Up the Moon, which had just come out the year before. I signed it to Sigrid and Hoken.

"You know about your great, great grandfather, don't you?" Hoken asked after a while.

"Do you mean that he named Randine as his mother on his immigration papers?" I replied. Hoken nodded. "It seems that the whole town knows that he was considered illegitimate. That story never crossed the Atlantic Ocean."

"Well, it is because of the Big Book, it just came out a few years ago. You know this?" Hoken said. "It is a big accomplishment this book."

"Yes, Mrs. Larsen told me. I did research on it at the University in Bergen when I was there over the last few days before I came to Laerdal. They gave me photocopies of the pages about the Lysne family. I am so excited to bring this information home to my family. And Randine, she was his wet nurse?"

"Yes, official wet nurse. Then on his immigration papers Henrik said she was his mother," Hoken said.

"She was probably the only mother he knew, as his mother must have died,"
I replied feeling a little defensive.

"Yes, and perhaps with her profession..." Hoken said.

"Profession?" What profession?"

"She was an official midwife, it says so right here," Hoken replied.

"Really! How fascinating."

"Mrs. Larsen had read that to me in the Big Book, but I had not taken it in. I couldn't help but wonder what would it have been like to be her in the 1820's and 30's? What a strong and independent woman she must have been."

The afternoon progressed as though we had known each other for many years. I had spent nine hours talking to my cousin and going over family history. We lost track of time. Tingles raced up and down both our arms when we realized that four generations had passed since our families were together in Norway. No one in our family lines had returned face to face until now.

"Four generations since Hoken left for America, and then his father also left a few years later with his entire family," Hoken said wistfully. "We were the ones that had to stay."

"And my ancestors were the ones who had to leave," I said quietly. "This was our legacy."

"Thank you Hoken. It has been just a wonderful visit," I said with gratitude overflowing. "It's getting dark. I guess it's time for me to head back to town."

"Wait," he said, "I have something for you."

As I stood inside the front door with his wife, I could not really speak to her, but gestured toward the house to convey how beautiful I thought it was. She smiled and said that Hoken had built it with his brother.

Hoken came dashing back with a box. It was an old shoebox, full of letters and several small books. As he lifted the cover Hoken said,

"These letters are not translated, but no one seems to have the time here since we can read the Norwegian! The letters were written to Randine by someone we do not know named Ursula. There are also copies of a journal of Randine's and some letters from Ola to her and his mother that I copied for you, as our family would like to keep the originals. If you see fit to take them on, they will teach you more about Randine, since you are so keenly interested in her life. She is not really related to our side of the family, more to yours. Of course they are written in Norwegian, these letters."

I stood for a moment looking at the box. It was an answer to my silent musings. What would it have been like to be Randine?

"Wow, thank you! What an extraordinary gift. I will cherish these letters."

After hugging Sigrid and Hoken and saying good night, I carefully placed the box of letters into the car seat next to me. But before closing the car door, I remembered an empty herring jar I happened to have in my purse that I carry vitamins in. I leaned down out of the car after empty- ing the jar and scooped up gravel and earth from the drive- way.

This earth is going on my altar. I thought, as I drove down the hill to my hotel.

Chapter One
Treasure

Bergen, Norway
Wednesday, 29 November 1820

Winds howled off the Bergen harbor as snow swept across the ice-laden dock and swirled around the Black Horse Tavern and the row of houses on the waterfront. Down the alley three blocks from the tavern, owned by Peter and Lena Erickson, was their other enterprise, Erickson's Bed and Board. Inside the boarding house, the Ericksons and young Randine and the other residents lay sleeping in their rooms, while the wind rattled the windows. A deep chill had set in that night as the temperature dropped with the incoming storm. The fires in the hearth had burned down to embers. It was just before dawn as Randine lay dreaming . . .

Thursday, 30 November 1820
Randine's Diary

That night before my baby came, I had a dream that Father came to my bedside and smiled at me, then Mother joined him. It was lovely to see us all together again, as though I had never been apart from either of them. As though there had never been that horrible fight between us. I felt so happy. They said nothing about James or how I was sup-posed to be their "perfect daughter." Nor did they ask me why didn't I just break their hearts completely by running away to marry him. Instead, they smiled calmly and with love. The bright colored lights of many spirits rose up behind my parents and gathered around my bed. These were the spirits of our ancestors and one, I know, was my dear brother. He was no longer the sickly tiny infant that had perished, but a full-grown man with light streaming around him. And then, my grandparents on both sides of the family came in to greet me. They, too, had light all around them. My grandparents died before I was born, but somehow, I knew them well. Their presence was comforting. The warm light flowed from them and encircled my bed.

Then James, my love, joined everyone. He looked sad, and yet was happy to see me at the same time. The light streamed from him like rays of sun through stormy clouds. He brought with him the power of the Norse Gods. Hella and Holda, the twins from the underworld, rested their cold hands on his shoulders. Then Mother Frigg and Father Thor came, too. Frigg, Goddess of the Hearth, had her spindle and her yarns. And Thor, with a stern but loving look on his bearded face, lifted his great arm and pounded his hammer on his golden anvil. Out shot a bolt of lightening that struck my belly. I screamed, waking myself up from the dream at once. I knew in that moment that James was dead.

Randine clutched her belly, seized by a spasm of pain unlike anything she had ever felt. She was terrified. She wasn't sure what to do, what to expect. Would she die? Would her baby survive? She wanted her mother—Mama! She would know what to do. She remembered this dream as though she were still in it, felt the stab of their absence, tried to hold on to an image of her parents loving her. But when she looked again, only Hella and Holda were smiling. Then the dream left her, and she found herself alone in her cold room in Erickson's boarding house. A spasm of pain broke through Randine's silent reflection and she screamed.

Mrs. Erickson shouted from the corridor, "Randine! Are you alright?" Dawn was breaking, the light through the window in Randine's room just enough to see Mrs. Erickson's shape at the door. She hurried over to Randine and drew back the heavy curtain shielding her bed from the winter chill.

Randine felt a bolt of pain, a kick, then a popping inside her, and a flush of warmth between her legs, as water gushed out of her.

"Get the midwife. Pleaaassse! It's time! My waters..."

Mrs. Erickson ran out of the room to rouse her husband.

"Peter!" Lena shouted down the hall. " Go and get the midwife. Randine is having her baby!!!"

Peter gulped down the last of his cup of coffee, grabbed his coat and hurried out the door. Then Lena flew back down the hall as fast as her large heavy legs would carry her, and climbed the stairs to Randine's room, lantern in hand. Randine could not move or sit up. The lamp played games on the ceiling, swirling light and shadows around the room, and a sudden sickness washed over her. She closed her eyes.

Mrs. Erickson sat by Randine's side on the low chair and took her hand to her heart and squeezed it tightly with both hands. Here was this young girl she had known since infancy, who needed all the support in the world, but there was no help for her because the church demands that people obey its moral law, then when people make mistakes it throws them out. It was no wonder why many parishioners practiced the old ways in the quiet of their homes. It was certainly why she and Peter would never step foot into any Lutheran church again.

Randine was still troubled by her dream, but Mrs. Erickson's face was warm and kind and she felt safe in her embrace. "I am scared, Mrs. Erickson."

"Dear, it is time you called me 'Lena.' 'Aunt Lena' if you prefer. Today you will become a woman for sure, and you should not call me as a child calls a neighbor lady. We are too close now for that."

"Lena, I'm scared."

"I imagine every mother is the first time. I lost all my babies. None lived. So Mr. Erickson— Peter and I—we just stopped trying. Then you came to me in your condition, and I felt as if you . . ."

Randine moaned as another contraction bolted through her body.

"Breathe, Randine, just breathe. You will be all right. Ursula has brought half of Bergen into the world. She will bring you and your child face to face."

Randine began to wonder if Ursula would ever come. She had known Ursula all her life. Everyone this side of Bergen knew Ursula. Then she wondered how she could pay for her service. She had no money at all. She worked for her keep, sweeping and scrubbing floors in exchange for her room and the meals at the boarding house table served by Mrs. Erickson every morning and evening, but she had not a penny of her own.

Lena patted Randine with her plump hand as she listed the names of all the mothers Ursula had attended in the past year. Just the sound of her voice eased the pain. Randine felt the baby kicking again, trying to get out.

"Calm down little one, you will soon be with us," she told her child. Mrs. Erickson brought her hand to her mouth to stifle tears.

"Ursula will be here any time now, dear. Don't you worry."

Just then, they heard voices on the street below and the crunch of boots in snow and ice. The bells hanging on a leather strap over the door rang merrily, and the front door creaked loudly. Happy conversation entered the house and up the steps to Randine's room. She could hear Peter greeting Ursula. Pain over came her again like huge waves rolling in from the sea. Randine could not restrain herself from screaming. Urusla's footsteps quickened. Randine kept seeing the faces of Holda and Hella. She couldn't stop crying to tell Lena.

Ursula brought the cold of the outside into the room on her coat. She had branches of spruce in her arms, and a basket of herbs and folded sheets and blankets. She looked at Randine and smiled. Randine's pain seemed to vanish at once.

"Oh Ursula, thank you for coming so quickly," Mrs. Erickson said.

"For Randine it must have seemed an eternity," Ursula joked, laying the branches down and stripping away the fronds. She handed some to Lena.

"Tea or a bit of coffee? It may be a while before the baby comes," Ursula said, watching Randine's face intently.

"I'll put the kettle on and make some barley meal for breakfast." Lena stood up at once wiping the branch leavings off her nightshirt. As she left the room she called after her husband.

"Peter, please bring up some wood for the fire. We will have a new child born in our boarding house today!" Lena sounded happy as she flew down the hallway and then the stairs, fluttering about like a nervous hen.

Ursula was now in her late thirties. Her brownish-blonde hair was tucked under a wool cap, tied gently under her chin to keep back the braid down her back. She wore a white pinafore over her grey-blue woolen dress and she had a watch pinned to her chest with a gold ribbon clasp. She was a stately woman, almost six feet tall, much bigger than Randine, with a straight back and broad shoulders. Randine noticed wisps of gray hair poking out under her cap, and the small lines around her sparking blue eyes. She was a handsome, hard-working woman.

"How are you feeling my dear? When did you have your last contraction?"

Ursula took charge at once. She wanted to see Randine's coloring. As Ursula drew the curtain wide open with one hand that separated Randine's bed from the room,

Ursula bent over to touch Randine's forehead and pat her cheek with the other.

Although the room was small, it was cozy. The fireplace was in one corner and her bed near the center of the rectangular room. A small window above the table and chairs at the end of the room by the door brought in the only natural light. Mr. Erickson brought in more wood for the day and set it down by the fire. Mrs. Erickson followed and brought in extra linens and an extra chair for their breakfasting.

As the Ericksons entered the room with their arms full, Ursula drew the bed chamber curtain closed around her and Randine. She then rolled Randine to one side while she removed the wet sheets. She laid down spruce branches over a straw-filled mattress then a clean sheet over the spruce. Ursula rolled the rest of the sheet in a long roll and tucked an extra cloth under Randine's bottom. As she was rolling Randine from one side to the other over the rolled up bed sheet, to dress the other half of the bed in the same manner, Randine tried to sit up, but Ursula pushed her back with a gentle hand.

"Just relax dear. You have a lot of work ahead of you."

After Mr. and Mrs. Erickson left the room, Ursula took a clean nightgown out of her bag and placed it over Randine's head. It was worn soft from years of use.

"This is my good-luck birthing gown that I always use to bring healthy babies into the world in Bergen. You are no exception. Come on now, everything will be fine. Sit up a little so I can remove the soiled one."

Swift and gentle as ever, Ursula stripped the old gown off of Randine and slipped the fresh one over her head. She was dressed and ready for labor.

"There now, you are just fine. Pretty as ever you are!" Randine's auburn hair was long and thick. Ursula brushed back a strand from her face. Since Ursula had known Randine all her life, and had brought her into the world, she was more of an auntie than a professional midwife to Randine.

Ursula began brushing her long hair and braided it and gave her a wash rag to clean her face and hands.

As Randine laid back, another jolt of pain ripped through her, and she cried out before she knew it.

"Breathe, Randine. Breathe. That's it, my darling. You are doing just fine."

Outside the cold north winds blew around the boarding house as sun rose above the sharp angled black roofs and white clapboards of Bergen. Icicles hung long along the gutters. No one was up yet at this hour but the drunks and the night watchman on board the Blue Pearl and Odin's Pride. Dark wool coats were brought up around watchmans' throats and buttoned up tightly as the grey sky lightened slightly and the harsh winds formed ice quickly on the roofs around the harbor. Snow swirls around the pathways and ice chunks formed on the harbor boats and the posts where the ships were tied up and rocking with the incoming waves.

The waves kept coming for Randine about every twenty to thirty minutes or so and she felt embarrassed by her loud groans with Mr. Erickson just below in their apartment. Who else was in the house she did not know. There was Mrs. Jensatter Knudson next door, a widow lady, who was barren and had no children, though still only in her thirties or forties. There was Mr. Larsen, an old man living out his days here at the Erickson's, and Mr. and Mrs. Swinholtz, who came down to Bergen from the north a few years ago after their son took over their farm. There was Miss Lily Olassatter, a retired schoolteacher. She was particularly skinny and very tall, like Ursula, but not at all a pretty women. She read most of the time and kept to herself. Randine did not like her, as she looked over her glasses with a disagreeable look and often shook her head in disapproval at Randine, as she grew larger. That was the usual supper table group at Erickson's Bed and Board. Though Randine had taken most of her meals in her room, she did not like the nosey questions and judgments from Miss Lily nor from the Swinholtzs. She vowed never be like them, lonely, stuck in their lives, and living out their days here until they die. She did like Mrs. Jensatter Knudson, as she was very kind and always greeted Randine with the concern of an aging aunt.

Finally the waves of contractions subsided.

"I am going to check to see if you have made an opening for the baby." Ursula said.

She lifted the dressing gown as Randine lay back, and looked for something she called her 'dilation.' It was not a word Randine knew.

"It seems that you have a ways to go Randine. Stay in bed and relax. Best not to eat, as you may throw it up anyway. We never know how long it will take for the baby to come. Do you want me to fetch your parents?"

Randine's dream returned again vividly. She paused. "I doubt if they would come, but I did dream about them last night. They were here, loving me. I felt their warmth."

Ursula nodded and looked at Randine with gentle eyes.

"At least let me send Lena to tell them. I am sure they would want to know, my dear." She didn't answer and turned her head away. Ursula changed course.

"Okay Randine, it is your choice." Randine looked back at Ursula when she began to describe the process of birth to her.

"Here is what will happen. This tightening you now feel will continue, and the waves of pain will get closer together. When the pains get closer and closer, you will know the baby is coming. You will feel it, and we will be sure that everything is all right before I have you push too much. Now, what about your parents?" Ursula asked again.

Randine could not answer, but just looked at her. Then she said, "I think they might make things worse."

"Okay sure, ya, it is your birth. What about Lena letting them know you're in labor?" It was more a statement than a question.

"Okay. But can't we tell them after it is all over?"

Ursula looked at Randine with her knowing look of a woman who had been through this a hundred times.

"They should know dear, you are just barely fifteen." Ursula drew the curtain back slightly. The heat from the fire warmed the corner now. "You are technically still their charge."

"Ursula, you know my mother. She is always storming around about something. She acts as if I did this to her on purpose. Father listens to her complaints and doesn't speak up, even though in private he often says he does not agree with her. I am caught in the middle as their only child. I only hear from her what I haven't done, how I don't measure up to her expectations for me. Now I have failed completely in their eyes." She started to cry, but managed to say,

"I don't want them here."

"As you wish, dear. We can at least let them know and ask them to wait for news. How is that? They will not come until after you have your child, I promise." Ursula said patting her hand.

"Okay, I can agree to tell them, but really, I cannot do this with them here."

"I will bar the door, dear. Now I must say to you, Randine, you are not a failure. You just got seduced!" Ursula looked at her as if she knew something Randine still did not understand.

"What does 'seduced' mean?" Randine asked her. Ursula put her head in her hands, and then, before answering, she pulled her chair closer and took Randine's hand in both her hands.

"It means you were lured into his trap. Some men can see a girl's innocence and use it against her, making promises they do not intend to keep."

Randine looked away, feeling ashamed. She knew James was not like that, but she could not find the words to speak up for him. She fingered the broken heart token that she wore on a string tied around her neck.

"He gave me this as a promise of his return," Randine

said quietly in defense of James.

Ursula sighed and said softly, "Yes, I see that, the oldest trick in the book."

"There is something we must discuss now while your contractions are calm. Randine, dear, have you thought about what you are going to do with the baby?" Ursula asked in a gentle yet firm way.

Randine turned her face to look at Ursula. "I-I don't know." Tears started again, and she could not help herself.

Randine knew what Ursula meant. How could she keep her baby? Unless her father would agree to provide for her at this boarding house, she had no other means of support. She would not be welcome to return home with a bastard child. Mother would not stand for it. She had to uphold her status as an upstanding woman of Bergen, wife of a successful merchant. Her good Lutheran friends would snigger and make life miserable for her. How could they treat their only daughter like anything but a tramp? Right now, no one but the Ericksons and Ursula knew she was still in Bergen.

"Ursula, I don't know what to do. My dream last night..."

Randine told Ursula about her dream of James and the others she saw. Randine's thoughts kept returning to her James. It was love at first sight. She remembered spotting him standing by the tavern door as she walked by with her father. His hair was dark as a raven and his eyes deep blue. He seemed different than the other men, as he was well kept and his high cheekbones were so rosy and when he smiled at her she said to herself and later wrote in her diary, That is the man I will marry one day.

"Randine dear, the first love is always the hardest. Who knows about James? He is not here to take care of you. I want to know about you. What are you going to do with yourself and with your child?" Ursula said those words as softly as she could. She knew most women assumed they would either marry or live with their parents the rest of their lives. Now for the first time Randine, at fifteen, had to think about herself and the baby apart from what was the custom.

Randine could not speak and felt the contractions increase. She sank into herself. Lena brought in a large tray and Ursula and Lena ate a quick breakfast with Mr. Erickson. The smell of the food made Randine feel sick. Ursula drew the curtain so she could rest as her contractions subsided. When they were finished eating, the women shooed Mr. Erickson out of the boarding house to tell Randine's mother and father she was in labor, but it would be best to let them know she was in good hands and not to come. She then asked him to find news of James, and whether his ship had made it through the storms. Other ships had returned to port damaged and in need of repair after the huge storm off the North Sea.

As soon as Mr. Erickson stepped out the door, Ursula peeked behind the curtain to see Randine was awake, then pulled it open wide to let the morning sun stream into the room.

"We will make this a woman's room now. It is a place just for you to bear this child into the world." She smiled, and the sun seemed to break with her calm. Randine sat at the edge of the bed. Then Ursula gestured to Lena, who took some dried flowers out of Ursula's bag. She placed the flowers in a wooden bowl, and added some cedar branches with dried seeds. Then she lit them with a coal from the fireplace, and blew out the flame. The smoke in the room smelled sweet and spicy at the same time.

"The lavender was brought to me from Scotland by my brother who sails there from time to time. He found them in a shop in Edinburgh. The woman shopkeeper said they help to clean the air, especially good for births."

"I am glad the flowers were from Scotland." Randine said wistfully.

Ursula paused and sighed. Taking the smoky flowers and crackling cedar branches in one hand, she waved them over Randine, then Lena, and then herself—being careful to catch any flying sparks with her other hand. She waved the smoking stalks throughout the room until they burned to the ends. The room smelled like flowers, and Randine felt lighter, and less afraid. Next, Ursula reached into her bag again and pulled out a little blue sack, out of which she pulled a round blue ball that looked like chalk, called 'woad.'

"This has been used by us midwives on the west coast of Norway since our people were Vikings. We got it from the Scots in the west across the North Sea, or they got it from us, no one can remember. It will help with the birth." Ursula lifted up Randine's gown and drew two symbols on her belly with the woad, then on each palm.

"Some men use woad to paint their faces before they go to war. Both the Scots and their Irish brothers did this when Rob Roy was trying to fight off the English in the last century. Now, this rune is the symbol for birth. It is called Berkana. This one, called Uruz, is for good strength and life force, health, and this one, Peorth, for release," she said. Then she made a circle with a cross around her naval. She explained that the Berkana rune was a 'B,' while the Uruz rune was an upside-down 'U.' Birth and strength, release. Randine took in everything Ursula said with great interest. She was one of the few educated older women she knew.

When Ursula was done, she put the woad back into the sack and brushed the blue dust from her apron. Randine pulled her nightgown over the woad markings on her belly, and patted them a little. Ursula took Lena's hand and Randine's hand to form a small, three-way circle.

"Let us say a little prayer for Randine and this fine baby. We ask the Mother God Frigg, to help our sister and daughter Randine in this labor. May she have an easy time. May you, Mother Frigg, guide my hands and Lena's to help her, and may we each feel the presence of the Sisterhood as we bring this child home. Twins Holda and Hella, guard the door and do not enter, so Randine can see her baby smile."

Never before had Randine had women pray over her like that. Could these women Gods she spoke of help instead of harm her? The Lutheran God seems so mean and punishing, and the Lutheran church sees people as nothing but sinners. Men are in charge, do all the praying at services and suppers; women have their sewing circles, but they do not pray together. Or do they? Randine wondered.

"Thank you Ursula. That was... so lovely. I didn't know women could pray with other women like that. I saw all of them this morning in my dream. Now I know, they have come to help."

Lena and Ursula looked at each other and smiled.

"Women have prayed together for centuries, my child. We do it in secret so the church fathers will not call us witches. But we do it for the good of all. When we are women with other women who know some of the old ways, it is safe. Who else beside your parents and James did you see dear, in your dream?" Ursula was leaning over her with keen interest, as she drew a chair closer.

"It was Frigg, with her staff, and Thor with his hammer. Thor threw a lightning bolt. That is when my water broke. The old ways... tell me about them. Tell me about the Goddess Frigg. Who is guarding our door, Hella and Holda?" Just then the pain got worse, and she was doubled over again.

When the pain left, the two women settled in close beside Randine's bed and began to tell stories. "Do not mention Hella's nor Holda's name again, while you are in labor, dear. They are goddesses of the underworld. Holda takes the dead babies home. She is not bad, she is very good, but she is not the one to call during labor," Ursula stated firmly.

Randine felt frightened for a moment, but pushed her fears away. Her baby would live.

"I saw them," Randine said.

Ursula looked at her so deeply she thought her eyes would burn right through her. To lift her spirits, Ursula began telling stories about other births.

"You know, Randine, I was an apprentice to Olga Tomasson Lars after Britta and I helped your own mother Anna bring you into this world. Later I will tell you all about it." For now she shared stories of other births along the Sognefjorden, that long stretch of ocean water that winds from Bergen 150 miles inland between high jagged mountains into the heart of Norway.

As they waited for the labor pains to get closer together, Ursula spoke of her training with Britta Tomasdatter Anders in the Sogn Fjord and with Olga in Bergen. She told of how she had followed these midwives from birth to birth for two years. When Olga asked Ursula to move to Bergen to help her, the two women lived nearby each other, and took turns taking emergency calls until Olga died ten years ago. Olga told her of herbs and flowers to use for births, teas to help ease the pain, and special salves. Olga left her house and her practice to Ursula after her death, and Ursula became the midwife for the whole of West Bergen. She was kept very busy, especially in the spring and summer. Ursula never married, but that was a story she did not want to speak about.

"It seems the population is growing, and I could use some help, I could," Ursula said. "But for now I am grateful for the strength of Berchta, the mother-creator, who gives us the work with women and children. She is the Earth Goddess, the keeper of the gate between life and death. Some say her rune, Berkana, the one for birth that I drew on your belly, was cast then danced around by the women of Christiania when they asked the gods to help them start a school for midwives there.

"A school for women?!" Mrs. Erickson said, startled.

"Yes, it has begun this very year, and soon some will be trained there first, then through apprenticeships back home in their districts if there are midwifes there already to share the work. The births themselves are the best training." Ursula affirmed.

Neither Lena nor Randine could take it in. Never before had women in Norway gone to school, unless their families were wealthy, and then only to Edinburgh or Copenhagen, which was often too expensive as someone would have to be hired to escort the girl to and from the school for their safety. The way of education most commonly practiced for girls was for the family to hire a tutor. Sometimes the tutor would teach several students at once in one of the houses. The child's education depended largely on the breadth of the tutor. Even then it was seen by most as a waste of money because the girl would end up bearing and caring for children. Now the government wanted women to train to be midwives and travel to Christiania? Peasant women at that?! Randine knew she had been fortunate, as her father had hired a tutor for her most of her life—until she became pregnant, that is.

Randine just had to walk around the room. She got up with the help of Ursula. Lena put some socks on her before she began pacing around in her soft nightgown. Randine asked about all the other women who gave birth in this gown. Lena wrapped her in a shawl. Then she stood by the fire until another contraction came and she was doubled over at the table again.

"Back to bed, now. You will be more comfortable there," Ursula commanded.

Hours passed. It was noon, although the gray skies concealed the sun overhead in the sky. Sleet hit the window of the room and an icy crust formed on the glass panes.

By late afternoon, the waves of pain were coming in like breakers. Randine, on her hands and knees on the straw mattress, was panting like a dog.

"This is good. Soon the baby's head will show. You are getting ready, Randine. That baby is coming soon." Ursula spoke as if they were taking a walk in the park. But her calmness was reassuring, and her gentle touch soothed Randine. She could not imagine going through this without her.

The sun was going down, and long shadows darkened the room. Lena lit the candles in the lamps.

"Twelve hours. It has been twelve hours since Randine began her labor," Lena reported, consulting the watch on a chain around her neck. She snapped it shut and tucked it back into the breast pocket of her dress.

"T'was a gift from my cousin Silva!" she smiled and patted her large chest. Lena wore sheepskin slippers in the house to cover her large feet. Randine wondered if they were really her husband Peter's slippers, as her feet were so large. She always had been a friend to Randine's family. Here she was again, being a guardian for her now, though sometimes she could create more harm than good. Ursula was watching something above Randine's head.

"Ok, Randine, now on the next one—push, and push hard—then we will see if you have a daughter or a son."

Suddenly, sweat broke across her body, as if a wave had washed over her. A contraction took hold and shook her body. Pain gripped her lower back and hips. Randine felt sharp needles of pain where the baby's head came through. She pushed as hard as she could, right through the pain.

"Breathe and push, Randine! You can do it." Ursula demanded.

"Holy Jesus, the baby is coming!" Mrs. Erickson shouted, squeezing her hands together.

Ursula supported own her back against the foot of the bed readying herself to catch the baby as it came out. Randine gripped the headboard, then her pillow, as Lena rubbed her lower back. "Here's the head... one more push... wait... wait for the contraction, Randine."

The sea subsided, and then she felt another wave rising from somewhere above her, rolling through her as a scream was released deep inside, so deep she did not know it was her scream. No doubt it could be heard all the way to the tavern.

Randine was grabbing the pillow, Mrs. Erickson, anything she could find. A slippery mass slid out into Ursula's skilled hands. All she could feel was that burning of the head pushing through and the waves washing every ounce of energy out of her. When it had past, she turned her head to see what Ursula and Lena were seeing.

"It's a boy Randine! You have a son." Ursula reported. She turned the baby lightly onto his side, and cleaned his tiny mouth so he could take his first breath. As he gasped, his color changed from bluish to pink. She turned herself towards Ursula and reached her arms towards the baby to look at him. Ursula lay the baby on Randine's belly with a blanket over him, the cord still attached. Lena was crying and grasped her hands and lifted them to the sky.

"Praise the Lord, Thanks be to Thor and Mother Frigg!" She said, over and over.

Randine sat up against the headboard to see the child better and Lena propped up a pillow behind her, as Randine lay back with her son.

"There, there, little one," Randine said sweetly to her son. She cuddled him in her arms and drew him between her breasts.

"Lay back, Randine. I want to check your bleeding," Ursula said with her commanding and gentle voice.

"Okay Mama, one more push. You need to birth the placenta now. When you feel the wave, push, and we are done."

Randine took a deep breath and pushed, and the warm red afterbirth slid out.

"Get some warm water in a bowl, Lena, please, and a washing cloth. Then please bring me another empty bowl."

Ursula's warm touch and practiced movements changed the sheet under her bottom, while Lena washed and wrapped the baby on the bed. He was calm and did not cry much. Ursula packed a clean cloth between Randine's legs to slow the bleeding. Then she tied the cord in two places with sinew. She placed the placenta in the empty bowl.

"Are you ready, Randine? Would you like to cut the cord?"

"I would like to ... yes, I think it is good that my son's mama do it—I brought him here, now I will free him from me to someday walk on his own two feet."

Ursula shuddered slightly, and her face looked serious for a second when Randine said this. She wondered why, but was so filled with joy that she didn't pay it much attention.

As the pulse ebbed and slowly left the cord, Ursula tapped the place between two pieces of sinew on the cord Randine was to cut.

"My darling child, I gave you life, and now I give you your freedom from my body. Bless you, first child of mine, I am so grateful, little lamb. I will call you James—the new James McGregor, Junior."

Ursula held the cord and guided the knife as Randine sliced it in two. She cut the tie that bound her baby to the placenta and set the baby free. He did not flinch, but kicked his feet as if to show he was eager to begin his walk from her. Ursula and Randine chuckled to see this. It was as if he had heard her prayer. After Ursula tied the cord close to his little body, Randine gathered her child in her arms.

"You know, the old ones say that the family, living and dead, gather when a new one comes through. It seems your parents came to wish you well even if they are not here in the flesh. They love you, Randine, in their own way."

All of Randine's anger at them was now gone. She knew they loved her and had come to show her in her dream even if they could not bring themselves to say it. Lena sent a boy to the Tavern to tell them of the baby's arrival.

Ursula cleaned the bed after shifting Randine and baby James into a rocking chair beside the fireplace. Lena took the placenta to prepare the stew.

"I will prepare the new mother's first meal with butter porridge! Then I'll fry the placenta and leave some for the father, too. It will bind them together as a family and make Randine strong again."

Lena took the placenta and laid it out on to the table where she began slicing it into pieces. She stopped for a moment and went over to Randine, hugging her long and hard.

"You have done what I could not. Thank you for giving us this gift today." Then she hugged Ursula, too. Tears streaked her face.

Lena wiped away her tears and returned to the

placenta and cut some onions and placed a few dried mush-rooms in water as she wiped her tears. She said that she had saved them for this special stew. Lena took a small fry-ing pan down from a hook on the wall near the fire.

"No onions, please Lena, just the mushrooms and the butter," Randine said, "I don't really like onions."

"If you please, could you make the butter porridge for her first? She needs her strength back," Ursula asked.

She put the mushrooms in the frying pan with some whale oil, and then added the chucks of placenta and they sizzled together. While Lena continued cooking, Ursula helped Randine back into bed and drew the curtain around the two of them.

"Now I will tell you the story of your birth, Rand-ine. When I was an apprentice to the midwife Britta, who I mentioned earlier, I helped your mother give birth to you in a little farmhouse on the Sognefjord. Anna's water broke in the boat they were sailing in, she and Haagen. The boat-man had to stop there because a storm was comin' in, and you, you Randine were coming, too. That day was much like today, stormy, but with hail the size of walnuts. The moment you were born, there was a clap of thunder, and an ava-lanche fell behind the barn! Right then I had a vision about your life that I will tell you about sometime. I knew we would be meeting again one day. But it is what your father said at your birth that I want to tell you now. He offered a prayer for you to be freed from the grip of your mother, just as you yourself said a prayer to give freedom to your son. Perhaps your father already knew how fiercely your mother held onto people she loves."

Randine was startled, but then she knew her father and how he was always cheering for her secretly as she grew up. In his own way, he was protecting her from her mother's gloom.

After a while, Ursula showed Randine how to feed the baby, and soon little James latched on without any prob-lem. Ursula chuckled.

"He is a hungry one, isn't he," Lena said.

"Oh, look at him eat!" Randine laughed.

Ursula promised to return the next evening to check on Randine and the baby. When she left, Randine began to drift off. As Randine looked at her son in bed with her, his shock of dark hair looked just like her James, and she was sure he would be proud of their son if only he were here. She fell asleep kissing him gently.

Chapter Two
The Terrible Fight

Sunday, 3 December 1820
Dear Diary, What a fine boy 1 have had. And James, where
are you now my love...

Outside, long shadows stretched over the icy streets.
But inside it was warm and cozy, as Randine nursed baby
James by the fire in her room. The Christmas season was
soon to begin. Randine was feeling lonely about this holiday.
She missed James terribly. It was their child's first Christmas. She had not seen her parents since they first learned
she was pregnant the previous summer.

As she nursed her baby, her thoughts drifted back to
the time when her parents first found out. By August it had
became obvious, as she could not hide her growing belly
any longer. No blood showed in her monthly rags and her
mother noticed this when Randine had brought her laundry
down for the maid to do. It was almost a relief when mother
had flown into a rage.

"Who is the father? This I want to know, this minute!" her mother screamed.

"I will not tell you, it is none of your —" Just then her
Mother slapped her face and screamed louder, "You expect
me to sit by while our only daughter sits there sayin' she is
pregnant by a man we do not know? And now you will not
tell us who is the father. You will tell me now. I demand it!"

"You do not know him, he, he is a sailor."

"Of course he is a sailor, who else who would beguile
you into bed? Certainly not a tailor, or the merchant Lar-
son's son, that is for sure. You could not be so lucky as that!
How could you do this Randine? Did you not think to find
a man with a decent living who could provide for you? You

have disgraced us with a common sailor, no doubt a second son! Dear God!"

Randine began to cry louder and more bitterly as if her heart would break, while her mother, Anna, wailed into her handkerchief. It was all too much. Just then her father, Haagen, over hearing the commotion, came into the front hall where Randine and her mother were arguing.

"Now Anna, it is not all that bad. We will have a grandson or granddaughter, and how wonderful. The son is sure to be a handsome fellow, and sailors, well I work with them all the time. They are not such bad fellas. Many of the seafaring boys come from good farms..." Her father Haagen cajoled.

"Not so bad! This is our only child, and now we have to be humiliated like this by a common sailor. It ruins our station, our standing in the community. After all the hard work you have done, Haagen, to get us our wealth and the respect of good folks. How dare you Randine!" Anna shot back.

"How dare you Mother!" Randine stood up and planted her feet under her. "Who do you think you are to put down the father when you have not even met him. He loves me, and he is a good sailor who, I might add, wants to take me to Scotland.

"SCOTLAND!" Anna wailed.

"How dare you care more about your status than me! I will not stay another minute in such a twisted home!" Randine turned sharply and stomped towards the door.

"Wait Randine, you cannot leave!" Her Father grabbed her arm. "Your mother is upset, but we love you. This is a problem we can manage together. Come sit, here. Tell us who the father is. We want to know so he will do right by you, so we know for sure he can provide for you," Haagen said pleading to his only daughter.

"SCOTLAND!" Anna wailed. "You can't choose a Norwegian sailor?!"

Randine wrenched her arm away from father's grip.

"You see that is all you care about, money, money, money. You do not care one whit about me, nor your grandchild. You do not even care if his father is from a good family or not. You do not care about anything but your stupid position. You can both go to blazes for all I care."

All she could feel was rage. Randine was so angry she walked straight out of the house. She did not stop to think where she would go or what she would do. She had walked all the way down Nøstertorvet Street to the harbor before she realized she had nowhere to go. Then the words her parents were saying began to make sense to her. "Provide for her," that was the last thing her father had said. How would she live, how would she survive? Randine sat on a bench in front of Ericksons' Tavern, tears streaming down her face. It was early in the afternoon, so no one was passing into the tavern as of yet. As she sat there, watching the ships unload their cargo on the dock, the sailors busy with their chores, her thoughts ran back to James. Was he back in Scotland now helping with the harvest? Would he return soon? She watched the ships and the other sailors working hard until Mrs. Erickson came by.

"Randine, what on earth is the problem? Why are you here sitting out in the dampness, and not at home?"

"I, I, left . . . home." She stuttered, sobbing.

"You left?! Good gracious, come inside and let us sit for a moment. We should talk."

Mrs. Erickson unlocked the pub and they stepped inside. "Why did you leave, my dear?" As she shut the door, Randine broke into a million pieces.

"I, I, I am going to have a baby!" She was bent over crying into her skirt. Mrs. Erickson's face was full of shock.

"A baby! I see, your parents threw you out?"

"No, I left. All they care about is their reputation. Mother said I was an embarrassment to them. It would hurt business. They don't care a whit about me or their grandchild." She could not stop wailing.

"Now Randine, I know that can't be true! Well, perhaps,

knowing your Mother's black moods. There now, dear, here is my hanky, stop crying dear, we have to sort this out. I will not leave you to the wolves, and neither will they, Randine. Come now, dry your eyes."

She blew her nose into the well-worn hanky that Mrs. Erickson provided her. Then she looked into Mrs. Erickson eyes.

"Mrs. Erickson, I cannot go back! Ever since my brother died, Mother, she has been horrible. She demands I do everything perfectly, she watches me like a hawk with every cold or sniffle. She does not want me to even walk to the store unescorted. Her moods are so black when she drinks too much, and then she says terrible things. My poor father and I have to listen to her drunken insults! I cannot go back to that house Mrs. Erickson. I cannot stand to live with her a moment longer. When I walked away, I felt free for the first time, as though I was walking out from under black cloud. I feel she is poisoning me and Father." Randine was telling as plain a truth as Mrs. Erickson had ever heard.

Mrs. Erickson sat back in her chair. "Randine, she's a poison to herself more than to you or your father. Loss is so hard on some folks. We can forget the suffering of the ones that's left behind. Your mother had great hopes pinned on your baby brother. The bereaved sometimes hold on too tight to the living and smother them. Your mother was so sorrowful after your brother's death. She had waited so long for another child, and like me has lost so many babies. But there's no one to blame but God."

"Randine, we will not let you fall, you will come stay with me. Here is what we'll do. I can give you this key to our boarding house. You go there ahead of me. There is a room upstairs where you can spend the night. Go and sit there and calm yourself, while I work at the tavern tonight. There's salt pork and a jug of milk on the kitchen table. You're welcome to it. Later we will make a plan, you and me and Mr. Erickson. Of course you will have to earn your keep. Are you willing?"

"Oh yes, I am a hard worker. I would love a chance to help. And I can read, too, and write, if you want letters done or help with figures. I sometimes help my father with his accounts." Her darkness lifted so instantly, it was like the sun had broken through the clouds and lit the room.

"My dear I will talk to your mother tomorrow. I shall see what we can mend together. By the way, who is the father of your child?"

"He is Scottish. James McGregor—from the clan McGregor!"

"Ah yes, we often see the Scottish sailors in the Tavern. Isn't Edinburgh the largest town there?"

"Yes, I think so. So he tells me. He is a good man, somewhat older than me—three and twenty or four and twenty. He is going to be a captain and serve on his own ship someday."

"Randine, everyone is older than you dear. Captain, huh. Randine, you are not
yet fifteen, he is ten or eleven years older? You won't be eligible until you are eighteen as is the custom. But here we are." Mrs. Erickson said and threw up her hands.

"I met him before Christmas last as we walked by your tavern. One day, when I was helping father with the accounts, James was carrying some of father's goods into storage from the ship. The merchants and the sailors help each other, you know. It helps their home ship and the sailors make extra money that way."

"James, isn't that a wonderful name? James was assigned by his captain to unload father's cargo from the ship when the weather turned bitter. It was last year, just before James was about to set sail for home for the holidays. I saw James often. Every day last fall, until the holidays again, when the men are released to go home. Father knew there was interest, but then there was interest from many of the sailors."

"Like dogs on the scent, they are to a young beauty like you." Mrs. Erickson smiled a wry smile and patted Randine's hand.

"When he returned again, that is when he began to ask to see me...court me. I would not tell him where we lived, and then one day, I told him he could come to visit me at my home. But Mother and Father would have objected because he was a sailor and he was not of means and I was too young for their approval. Last January, he climbed the outside garden wall to my room. He came just that night, and we only talked quietly so my parents would not wake up. He was a gentleman, never asked for a favor from me. I had never met someone so warm and loving...then he left on tour again. When he left I thought my heart would break. He came back after Ash Wednesday, to the trellis and threw stones at my window and I let him in. That was the first time I saw him since the end of January, the month before... He gave me a necklace with a coin broken in half. He had one half, and I had the other. He said I was to keep it until I came of age, and he could then marry me. I thought he was proposing, a pre-engagement. I think that was the night we bundled, and that first time, we conceived. Before that night we had only slept together with our clothes on just once, and we kissed.

"He is so tall and handsome. I know he has the reputation that goes with the sailor, but he is different than the others. He did not approach me right away. He took his time, and did not ask to see me at night until many months had passed. I know he will come back again, but now he will not know where to find me." Randine began to cry again.

Mrs. Erickson had arisen from her seat and was pacing about the room as she listened to Randine explain about their courting.

"Oh, for the love of God, nothing is worse than a patient sailor. I wish they educated young women in the ways of the sailors. The broken token—that is the oldest ploy for winning favor I have ever heard—Holy Mother of God, if I have heard it once, I have heard it a hundred times!"

"Look Randine, I hope you are right about Mr. James McGregor, this unknown sailorman. At least he is from good land. Scotland is practically Norse after Eric the Red; they are like cousins to us. Mother Norway, as you know, belonged to Denmark until a few years ago when we declared our independence. Of course those rats-the Danes gave us to the Swedes. How could they do that! But thank God for our new constitution. It will lead to independence. You wait and see!"

Mrs. Erickson had strong political opinions, as she had seen many changes from her tavern windows as she watched the various countrymen come and go in the busy port of Bergen—mostly Scotts, Germans, Swedes, and Danes.

"Randine, believe me when I tell you many a good young woman has been taken in by the broken token. It is the oldest ploy of a sailor in the book. I can see just why your mother is upset. It's only a few years back she lost your brother and now she's afraid of losing you."

Randine thought of her brother, her tiny little brother, who only lasted three days. He looked fine in the cradle after he was born. She remembered how at ten, she had to stretch up on her tiptoes to see him over the side of her parent's bed when her mother changed him.

But something was wrong and everyone knew it. The little fellow was in pain, and he cried and cried. He could not drink mother's milk and when he did, he spit up most of it. There was something blocking the digestion in his belly, or so the doctor said. But after three days of trying to feed him, and being up all night with his crying, mother went to feed him one more time, and found him cold and dead. It broke Mother's heart.

"They had tried so long to have another child, Randine, you were already ten years old." Mrs. Erickson recalled.

"The minister came to our house to baptize him the night he died." Randine remembered.

In 1816, the year after her brother died, the winter never ended and summer never came. It snowed well into May and the growing season ended early, on the first of

August. It was cold for most of that summer. So little of the harvest survived there was not enough to eat. Even if you had money to pay, there was no food to be had. That was the year when Randine turned eleven, and she thought for sure her mother must have been controlling the weather with her dark moods. It always went from gray to black with Anna, nothing sunny and bright. And so it was with the endless snow and frost that surrounded Bergen. Randine made up her mind that she would never be like her mother, and now that she was about to be a mother herself, she did not want her sadness to darken her baby's life.

The sailors of Bergen had heard from the sailors they met in Christiania and Copenhagen that a volcano had erupted somewhere on the other side of the world in the late spring of 1815. Randine remembered that as her mother's hope for another child faded, she withdrew into the dark mountain of herself. The weather grew colder and colder and summer never came.

Anna became more religious after her loss, certain that she must have terrible sins to atone for. She became a member of the Ethics Society at her church, which took a dim view of immoral behavior, and visited people who seemed to be outside of the Christian norm. She blamed herself for her son's death and pushed all her grief down inside herself, but it came raging out at Randine and her father when she got drunk. Randine's father followed his wife's lead into piety and drunkenness, and there they were, caught in the idea that God punished them with death and that life on earth was rewarded with salvation in heaven. It was a concept that always confused Randine. She didn't like that belief one bit. That is when she left her parents in her heart, and when she left the church in her mind.

Her brother's death was the beginning of the end of Randine's childhood. There was no joy in the house after that, and she looked away from her family life for the first time, realizing that she would not stay with her parents any longer than she had to. It was then that she decided to grow up, move beyond her parent's grasp. The desire for escape is what burned in her when she first met her lover, James a few years later. He was her way out, when he asked to court her in the middle of the night. She became pregnant four months into her fourteenth year.

Back in her room at the Ericksons' Bed and Board, Randine held her son, who lay sleeping in her arms. Randine would not be like mother, no matter what. She knew that her own babies would be healthy, she was sure of that.

The next day, everyone in Bergen heard of the Scottish ship that went down in the North Sea trying to return to Bergen. It was James' ship and all on board were lost. When Ursula came to check on how Randine and the baby were doing, Ursula told Randine of the terrible loss. Randine would never see her James again.

After Ursula left Randine she sat there terrified after hearing the news. Randine knew in her heart that she could not keep little James. How could she provide for her son without a father? Her heart ached as she watched her darling son. When the baby had eaten his fill, she changed his diaper. She talked to little James about his father, who came "from far across the sea." Then she slept for a while with her baby again.

The next afternoon, after putting on clean clothes, Randine found herself getting the baby ready, too. When she heard her neighbor, Mrs. Jensatter Knudson, return from her dress making shop, Randine gave her time to settle into her room. Then Randine found herself being pulled to her neighbor's door. It was as though the hand of angels were guiding her there.

Before she knew it, Randine was knocking on Mrs. Knudson's door. The kindly woman opened it to greet Randine, and smiled when she saw the child. Before she could say a word, Randine kissed the bundle in her arms, took a deep breath.

"He has been fed. His name is James, James Mc-

Gregor, descended on his father's side from the clan Mc-Gregor," she said. "I changed him too. He is a good baby, I am but fifteen and cannot keep him, will you care for James?"

Mrs. Jensatter Knudson smiled though her eyes were sad and filled with compassion. She nodded and reached out for the child.

"Randine, are you sure?" Mrs. Jensatter Knudson asked as she received the bundle. "What about your parents?"

"I am his mother, full-blooded Norwegian both sides. Born Randine Haagensdatter Stokanes Luster... My parents do not want him, his father went down in the Scottish ship, I have no means...Before she could finish speaking, she began to cry, handed her darling son to her neighbor and turned away.

"Thank you, dear, I will take good care of him. What a blessing..." Mrs. Jensatter Knudson called after her. She closed the door and Randine never saw her son again.

Chapter Three
Broken

Tuesday, 5 December 1820
Dear Diary, Oh, my heart is so broken, James ship is lost and my son, is not my child any longer…

Ursula got a note through an errand boy from Mrs. Jensatter Knudson the next day. That is when she discovered that Randine had already given the baby to Mrs. Jensatter Knudson. After checking with the new mother to see if she needed a wet nurse and to arrange getting supplies for the baby, Ursula returned to Randine's room and found her packing her things to return to her parent's house.

"Dear are you alright?" Ursula asked Randine.

"It is better this way," Randine said but did not look up.

Randine sat on the bed, sobbing inconsolably over the loss of her lover and her newborn son. She begged Ursula to help her find another way than to return home to her parents.

"Ursula, I cannot go back to Mother's, I just can't, now that James is dead."

As Randine pleaded with her, Ursula fell silent, but then her eyes brightened.

"Randine, why don't you come help me for a while with other births. It would be good for you, and I need so much help with washing the sheets and mending."

Randine went from total despair to radiant hope. She jumped at the chance to help Ursula with her midwife duties.

"Ursula, I could really come work for you?" Randine leapt off the bed and hugged her.

After helping Randine check out of the boarding house,

Ursula took her to her own tiny house down the street to a few blocks away. The small blue house had white trim and a small porch on the front with a bay window. As they walked in Randine saw a table in the bay window with chairs around it, and built in bench seats under the window. The stove and kitchen were just beyond it. To the right as they entered Randine could see a ladder above the kitchen and the living room.

"There is a bed up in the loft, where you can sleep to-night. We will figure out your chores tomorrow."

Randine sat down on the rug beside the fireplace and wept bitterly. She touched the love token that she wore on a string around her neck, and rocked back and forth as Ursula sat in the rocker next to her and rubbed her back. Ursula just let her cry it all out.

A few days later, after breakfast, they heard a knock at the door. A delivery boy handed her the note. "Come quick, Ursula," the note read. It was signed, but Ursula did not say whom it was from.

Before she left, Ursula made some tea for Randine and gave her a slice of cake, and she showed her where the sheets were for the bed in the loft. When Ursula returned several hours later, she woke Randine, who was fast asleep in the rocker by the fire.

"Look what I have brought you, dear."

Randine rubbed the sleep from her eyes, and heard the cries of a baby.

"He is hungry Randine. Will you feed him? His mother died in labor just a few hours ago," Ursula said sadly.

Randine looked surprised. But she sat up and unbuttoned her blouse without giving it a second thought. The baby nuzzled her breast, and she suddenly found herself with a new charge.

Chapter Four
The New Father

Friday, 8 December 1820
Dear Diary, Today is the first day of my new boy's life... I
cannot understand this world one tiny bit, can you? ...

Ursula watched Randine with this new baby over the next day or so. She could see the questions racing through her mind. But she was also engaged with this newborn boy. She wanted to care for him—that much was plain. Two days later, after Ursula had returned home from a call, she sat down to talk with Randine.

"Randine, the baby's father is in port. His ship came into town not long before the child's mother went into labor. It was he that sent me the note from his sweetheart's bedside. When I got to the house she had given birth but was beyond helping as she had all but bled out. Still the baby was alive. He said his good-byes to his betrothed, and I promised him I would find him a wet nurse. He wants to come and see the child again, and meet you, Randine . . . before he goes back out to sea."

"Am I to be the child's wet nurse permanently? How does..."

"If you want to be, yes. The father will provide room and board and a little money for you to buy food and whatever you might need for the child. He is a sailor for the Royal Norwegian Navy. He cannot care for the child anyway in the first year or so, as a child that young needs a mother and he will be away at sea. We can talk about details later."

The next evening, Ola got relief from his night watch with help from his friend Paul to visit his newborn son. Since Ursula's house was only blocks from the harbor, Ola walked the short distance to her house. He stepped onto the porch of Ursula's house, his cap in hand, and knocked briskly. When Ursula opened the door, he tried to hide his feelings with a smile, but his sad, weary eyes spoke the truth.

"Come in, Ola," Ursula said warmly.

As he entered the tiny house, bending his head under the door frame, Ola could smell the scent of lavender and birthing stew, then he heard the little cries of his son, and knew that something in him had changed forever. His sad eyes filled with so much love at the sight of his son, though his joy was mixed with grief for the loss of Ragnild, the child's mother. Ola knew that they would always be together in spirit, he and Ragnild, and he must accept things as they are.

At twenty and five, he was the picture of the Norwegian Sailor, extremely tall, almost 6'5," and extremely handsome, with high cheekbones, fair skin, and sky-blue eyes. His shock of dark brown hair was raked to one side. Even in the dim candlelight, Ursula could already see a few white hairs on the sides. His dark blue uniform was neat, his shoes polished—and of course, he wore his government issued, double-breasted wool coat to keep him warm in the freezing weather outside.

"Come in, Come in," Ursula said, "quickly, so the child and mother will not catch a chill."

When she escorted this strapping, though humble, young man to the fire, he gasped when he saw Randine with his son. Here was a beautiful young woman, her long hair, the color of red autumn leaves, falling around her shoulders, with his son nestled in her arms. Ola could not help that his knees buckled as he folded himself into a chair beside her and the baby. Randine was radiant. Her fiery beauty and love for his tiny boy felt to him like the morning mist at sunrise. So too, he felt this woman's sadness.

Overwhelmed, he looked down at his hands. When he lifted his head to look again, and touched his little boy's hand, he said a prayer out loud that no harm come to his

son, or to this woman. He received an answer in the inno-
cent scent of his son's breath. He prayed that his son would
grow to be a fine man.

Ursula could see by the look on Ola's face that he was
struck by Randine's beauty, all the more amazing when she
herself had labored to bear a child only a few days before.
Fate had brought them together. At this moment he did not
even know her name.

Randine's eyes were filled with tears that spilled
over and streaked her face, as she looked first Ola, and then
his tiny son. She did not utter a word. She could not. Ursula
introduced them.

"Ola, this is Randine Hakonsdatter Stokanes Luster;
Randine, Ola Tomasson Lysne, from Laerdal.

"I-I named the baby Henrik. Is that well for you, Miss
Stokanes Luster?" Ola said cautiously.

She could only nod, and attempted a quivering smile.
Ursula felt so for her. Here she was, only fifteen, and already
with a loss of such magnitude it would have paralyzed or
driven many a young woman mad. Within a few days, losing
her own lover and having to surrender her own son—leaving her with breasts full of milk and no one to love.

Ursula served them each a bowl of the stew for new families from the placenta that Ursula had saved from James
that Lena made, mixed with the placenta from Henrik's.
While they ate they watched Henrik sleep in her arms. That
night after the stew was gone, Ursula invited Ola to stay the
night with them.

"It would be good for the two of you, and good for your
son as well," Ursula said.

Randine settled in to Ursula's bed in the back of the living for the night while Ursula retrieved bedding for Ola. Ola
unrolled the blanket on the floor next to her bed without
saying a word. Ursula returned with her bedroll too, as she
knew that tonight Randine might need some help. Ursula
wanted to be sure that this new family got off to a good
start.

Twice in the night the baby woke, crying for more food or the changing that he needed. The three of them got to know one another that night. When the baby woke with the mother's movements, Ola woke up too. Then he would watch her nurse until the baby fell asleep again. Ola could see her face in the moonlight that streamed through the frosted windows. He got up to stoke the fire both times, putting a log or two on to help the heat rise a bit.

"These first days of December are so cold. I hope we do not have too much snow this year," Ola whispered to her.

She was busy watching her new charge, and studying his every movement, still in awe of the birth of this new life. She felt as if this child was her own. She could not let in the pain of her loss.

"It will be what it is. Cold or not, I will be warm with Henrik," she replied, without looking at Ola as he tended the fire.

"We need to talk of a plan," Ola said quietly.

"Løytnant (Lieutenant) Lysne, we barely know each other. I must catch up with all of this. I cannot even take in my loss, and this new gain." She pointed to Henrik, and her tears overtook her. She cleared her throat.

"Let us talk of this later, please, it is just too soon, I-I can't."

Ola felt the door of their conversation close behind her statement, and watched as she scooted down into the remaining warmth under the covers. The baby was sleeping by her side.

Then, as if to buck himself up from the depth of sorrow, he said quietly with forced cheer, "You are right, come on, let us sleep. For now, I will protect you and the child from the Herderers."

Ola folded himself into his blankets on the floor beside her, with his back to the curtain that surrounded her bed facing the fire. She faced the fire and the curtain, which she had opened slightly to welcome more heat. Henrik was tucked in the curve of her body.

He could love her if she let him, thought Ursula, who lay awake much of the night. This was already apparent to her. Herderers--Yes, protect her and the baby. To Ursula, Herderers were merely a folktale, she-cows in search of a healthy baby after they lose their own. But she knew that the fear of the common people was real. Many Norwegians believed that if the men did not protect the women and children adequately in the first days, the Herderers would come in the night and steal their newborns. Sometimes they would replace them with their unhealthy or dead babies.

In the morning, Randine and the baby lay sleeping. Ursula awoke and took one look at Ola's face and motioned for them to move to the kitchen. Then she asked him in a whisper,   "What is the matter Ola, you look confused??"

Replying in a hushed voice he said, "No, no, it's nothing--well, . . . let's have some breakfast and I will tell you over the breakfast. Is there any coffee?"

He rose to stoke the fire and get it blazing again, and stir the pot of porridge, but first he drew the heavy curtain around Randine and Henrik to let them sleep as long as possible. While he stirred the pot over the flames, Ursula could tell that he was also stirring his thoughts.

Sitting down to breakfast, he told Ursula of the dreams he had in the night. He spoke of dreaming about his home. What he saw in another dream was very disturbing to him.   "There was Ragnild, as happy as ever, entering a dark room, and as she went away she handed him their child. He held onto the baby, and then she was gone. Next he saw Randine standing there beside him, and she took Henrik to her breast, and walked away. Then I woke up."

"I can't let this happen, Miss Ursula, I want Henrik and ... Randine in my life." Ola looked at Ursula with a mixture of fear and desperation in his face. All she could do was squeeze his hand. Then she offered some encouragement.

"Give this time, Randine will come around."

Ola stayed late into the morning. He heard Randine stirring behind the curtain as Henrik fussed a bit. When she opened the curtain she was ready to get out of bed, and eat, too. He watched her eat Ursula's butter porridge and feed the baby. When Henrik was done Randine put him on the bed to sleep, and wrapped him in a blanket to keep him warm. Ola was relentless.

"Miss Stokanes, we must talk."

"Randine, please, call me Randine."

"Randine. We must make a plan..."

"I cannot talk about any plan just now, Løytnant Lysne, please. I will tell you when I might be ready to speak with you. But I cannot talk of it now."

"Please, call me Ola. Let me at least say that I want to support you and Henrik, but I make so little as a sailor, I cannot support you well on your own here. In the country it is different as my family lives in a farm community, a gärd, where we work together to help each other survive the winters. In my valley, there is our farm, my mother and brother run it. Mother will help you take care of the baby while I am gone aboard ship. You need a place to eat and sleep, my farm can provide this for you; the farm, my brother and mother they will help as well as the cotters."

"Ola, please. I know there is much to talk about, but I cannot do it right now. Please."

"I know this is not what either of us dreamed of. But I feel it is my duty to marry you as soon as I have enough money to buy us a small cottage, and as soon as you are of age–eighteen, at least. That is the age in the country when women marry in Laerdal, eighteen or twenty, but before that, it would look suspicious for us to marry. So we cannot go home to Laerdal unless we think of a way to disguise the birth of your son. We shall intend to marry within the next year."

"Ola, please stop! I cannot think about all this." Randine was almost shouting at him now. Her angry voice woke up Henrik and he started to cry. She was not like Ola's passive lover, Ragnild. Randine was strong, and she was not going to be managed or pushed around. Her heart was so broken she could not discuss another thing.

Ursula watched Ola back peddle right out of the conversation. Randine was fuming with anger. But there was something else going on, and Ursula wasn't sure what it was.

Randine was shouting now. "I know I am as upset as you. You and I will have ...I am your son's wet nurse, and that is all. There is nothing else to think about right now. Can't you see?"

They had forgotten about Ursula even though she was in the same room with them. She had been dozing in her chair near the fire until the shouting woke her up.

Randine got up and threw open the curtain to pick up Henrik before Ola could stop her. Ola had not experienced a woman's wrath before this, and knew that she had good reason to be upset. The baby started to cry a full-on cry now.

Ursula knew she had to interrupt. Ursula cleared her throat to speak, "Ola, Randine—
Dear you look like you swallowed a fishhook, calm yourself, you will sour your milk, you are upsetting the child." Ursula said playfully to lighten the air a bit.

"I have? Oh no, I cannot poison him. Please come help us, Ursula. Here, you take him. Maybe you can help us figure this something out." Randine begged. She was a puddle of guilt and shame and would do anything to make this all go away. All she could do was sob.

Ursula put her hand up signaling that she did not want to take him. Instead she turned to Ola.

"Would you like some bread and tea? It is from yesterday but it is still quite good." Ursula suggested, looking at Ola and leaving Randine with Henrik.

"Yes, thank you, I would love tea, and a small slice of bread, something warm, winter is setting in, can you feel it?" Ola said trying to be cheery.

"So, how can I help?" Ursula stated in her no non-sense way.

"I feel we need to make a plan, for Henrik, for Randine." Ola pleaded.

"NO, I cannot be a part of any plan. I haven't even said good-bye to James and my own child. My baby is bundled in the arms of a new mother, and the bodies of the sailors they recovered are lying with the other bodies of people waiting for burial in the spring in the boathouse. Can't you understand! How can I speak of a plan with..."

"Now dear, settle down, you really will sour your milk if you don't control your anger. Your new son will pay with an upset tummy." Ursula said this so flatly that she stopped Randine's rant in mid-sentence as she held Henrik tightly.

"Yes, Randine, you are right. Ola, I understand your need to protect your son, too. But Ola, there is no hurry. Randine will not run away with your child. She is here, and will be here for sometime. When do you leave again?"

"I leave for Laerdal before the next full moon, the week before Christmas. That is only two weeks away. I wish to make a plan I can take home to my family. I want to tell them of the tragedy, tell them what happened to Ragnild, tell them of Randine."

"You can do all that without a plan. Randine is the wet nurse. That is all they have to know. Leave it at that for now. She has had to endure much in these past days. Ola she is just fifteen, and it has all been too much for her. Give her a little time."

"F-fifteen?" Ola said.

"Yes, Ola, fifteen. You make your plan, but keep it to yourself until she can reconcile all of this. You have to grieve, too, you know. Go and see her body. She is laid out in the boathouse with the rest. It will bring home your loss."

"This will take time for Randine. Let her feed Henrik and bond with the child. Let her become the mother of this boy, and then she will feel like going anywhere that is best for him. Do you see?"

"I had no idea she was just 15." Ola found himself sitting down to take in the news.

Ola understood Ursula, but Randine could see that his pride was hurt. He just wanted to do his duty by providing for his child and Randine.

'Thank God he is such a man!' Ursula thought. Then Randine did a remarkable thing. She asked Ola to get comfortable. Then she placed his son in his arms.

"Put him next to your throat and face so he can smell you, Ola," Ursula suggested.

Ola was transfixed as he held his boy for the first time. He looked into the child's sleepy face, and said hello. Then he did as Ursula suggested and the child settled down. He lowered his child so he could see his face and stared gently into his eyes.

"I am not going anywhere. It is dangerous even to take him out of this house in mid-winter. So do not worry. We have lots of time." Randine spoke to him more calmly now, though her chin quivered as she spoke. She ventured a smile and placed her hand on his shoulder.

"We'll talk when you are ready," he said. "I will be in the harbor for a week or so, then I'll be back before I leave for the Christmas season in Laerdal," Ola said, and handed the bundle of his child to Randine. "May I come tomorrow? I have a friend who will cover my night shifts."

"Yes, of course, come when you can." Randine ventured a smile.

"I must get back to the ship. The watch will be changing soon."

He rolled up his blanket again, then snapped to attention and clicked his heels together; he dipped his cap to them both and left the house with a little rye smile.

Ursula helped Randine back to bed and under the covers and tucked her in.

"Just rest Randine. Nothing has to be decided today. You have plenty of time. Leave Ola to his knowledge of his hometown. Then follow what he says. He knows the ways of the farming folk. You do not. These rural farms are not like Bergen. No, not like the city at all. You will see."

Randine waved her hand to indicate quiet, please. She was too tired to say another word. As she crawled into the bed she rolled away towards the wall, Ursula laid the child in next to her. He began to suckle again. Randine caught Ursula's hand as she withdrew it from the child and squeezed it gently. Randine's eyes were deep and full of tears. Ursula smiled at her.

"It is going to be all right, dear," Ursula said softly stroking her hair. "I promise."

Randine could hardly keep her eyes open, as her new son stopped nursing and they were both asleep again.

Chapter Five
The Visit

Monday, 18 December 1820
Dear Diary, You are not going to believe who came to visit
me today...I was shocked to see them again, how this time has
taken a toll on all of us...

Since she had come to Ursula's to stay Randine's only visitor was Ola, with the exception of Mrs. Erickson from time to time. Ola had come and gone from Ursula's house many times in the days that followed, and he had not said another word to Randine about his plans for her and Henrik. He wanted to give her the time she needed, and he had to think about how to tell his family. Randine was getting Henrik dressed when she heard a knock at the door.

Thinking it was Ursula whose arms would be full of dirty sheets from the birth she just attended, Randine bundled Henrik in his blanket and laid him in his cradle beside the fire Ursula had borrowed the cradle from a woman with several children living just down the street.

When Randine opened the door she was shocked to see her parents standing there. Randine stared at them at first as though they were strangers then stepped aside and welcomed them in.

"Mother, Father, please, come in." Randine said with a great deal of caution.

While they entered the warm house she noticed that both her parents looked older. She had not seen them since the day she left home four months before. Now they had come. 'This was at least a new beginning,' Randine thought.

Randine led her parents over to the cradle to see to her sleeping son, and showed them his tiny hand curled around her finger.

"He is a wonder, isn't he, I am so grateful for his life!" Grateful to the goddess, Frigg, she thought, though she kept this to herself.

"He is precious, Randine, just as you were, and your brother, God rest his soul," her father, Haagen said softly.

Her mother was silent, then placed a hand on Randine's shoulder and turned her around to receive an embrace.

"Randine, I am so sorry that I was not there for his birth. Forgive me, daughter." Her Mother said. Randine realized Ursula must not have told them of baby James's adoption.

"You are forgiven, Mother, and I am truly sorry for my harsh words before I left. Come sit by the fire, I'll bring him, too, as it is a bit chilly if we are not near the hearth."

Randine's father brought over a chair from the kitchen table, and the three of them sat together, looking at the flames. Randine wondered what they were thinking, as she felt the heaviness of their presence. It felt like more than guilt that brought them here to see her. This was a good start to end the argument they had in the past.

"It is time, that you knew who the father is," Randine said, hoping to break the remaining ice. "His father is a good man from Laerdal, his name is Ola Tomasson Lysne."

"Ola, I do not recall Ola. The one who helped me in the warehouse these past two summers, that was James McGregor from Scotland, was it not?" Her father asked.

"Yes, he is the one. Well, it is Ola, too. Let me explain. That is where James and I met father. James was the sailor that helped you in the warehouse; while I took care of your accounts as we unloaded stock, remember?" Randine replied.

"My God, Haagen, did you not keep an eye on them? Are you not the father of a beautiful daughter who you must keep from the wolves?" Anna said as loudly as she dare, so as not to wake the baby.

"He is not like that, Mother, we courted for some

time. Wait. Let me explain. You might as well know. James and I night-courted last February, before—before, he stayed the night with me," Randine, said hesitantly. "He thought I was years older than I am."

"How did he get in? What wall did he..." Haagen said, surprised. "You let him in?"

"It does not matter now, but if you must know, he threw rocks at my window, and I went down to the kitchen door and let him in," Randine explained, feeling impatient with their questions. "It was just one night."

"Lysne, I knew some Lysne's from Laerdal when I lived in Årdal. It was just at the end of the fjord. His father and brother are farmers?" Anna asked, sensing her daughter's discomfort, and changing the subject.

"Wait, there are two men. Yes, Ola, Henrik's father grew up there. Ola's father Tomas died some time ago, when he was three or four, and his older brother Knut Tomasson Lysne runs the farm now. Ola is planning to go back to Laerdal eventually, where his family can get to know Henrik. He wants to get transferred to the Army instead of being in the Navy, hopefully stationed in his hometown." Randine cautiously stated, "But James, he was the father of my son. I gave him away to Mrs. Jensatter Knudson when I had no way to care for baby James." Randine's voice trailed off.

"You are leaving Bergen? When is that?" Her mother's surprised tone was much sharper now.

"We don't know yet, it may be sometime. Mother, I lost him. My own child's father James was lost on that ship that went down...and I gave our baby to Mrs. Jensatter Knudson because I couldn't care for the child alone. When I heard the news about James, it made sense that I let our child go. Now I am the wet nurse for Henrik. Ola is his father, and the child's mother, Ola's lover, died at the birthing. Do you see? We have some time before we make any plans for the future." Randine said with certainty. "I only met Ola a few times so far."

Her parents were silent for sometime. "Oh, my dear child," Anna said, and threw her arms around her daughter. Then her father said slowly, "Wait, Randine, you lost your lover and your son has been adopted by whom? When did this happen?"

Randine was crying again and felt her mother's loving presence like never before. As angry as her mother had made her in the past, at this moment she was as loving as a mother could be.

The three of them settled into silence. Then her father began slowly. "We have talked, your mother and me, of moving back to Sogndal near Laerdal to start a small hotel there. The fishing is so good in that region. We could easily have meals for the guests. It would not be in Laerdal, but close by, in Sogndal or Årdal, down the fjord."

Randine did not speak, but rose from her mother's embrace. She checked Henrik's diaper and tended to his blankets, drying her tears. She moved as if her father had not floated out a proposal of solidarity.

"Do what you wish, it would be nice to have you close by—that is, if I do decide to marry Ola—of that, I am not yet sure. But I must tell you, I will not be able to be Ola's wife for sometime. He is gone a great deal away at sea. I do not know if I even like him. There is no talk of that now, as he is too busy with his post and must do well if he is to be promoted. His family is willing to support me on the farm until he is more stable. But for now, I...I will be going on as Henrik's wet nurse.

"What?! Just a wet nurse? That is a great sacrifice, if you do not intend to wed. Why won't this man marry you right now?!" Anna was clearly disturbed. "What is this excuse, about his promotion? I don't believe it. Who does he think he is..."

Henrik started to fuss with his grandmother's angry tone.

"Now dear, stop a moment and think. Randine going back to Laerdal without a formal proposal might buy them the time he needs to gain a greater rank and pay, too. You know how little they pay the sailors," Haagen said, trying to soothe his wife's frustration.

"I had such hopes for you Randine, and now, now you will be the wet nurse to a man who is a common sailor, instead of..." Anna began to cry.

"I am sorry your plans for me did not work out the way you wanted Mother, but perhaps you should have consulted with me before you laid them. This is my life, and yes, I realize my errors. But here we are, Henrik is my son now, and I will do anything for him, just as I am sure you would have done for Torsten, God rest his soul.

"It is my fault that Ola will not marry me. He did ask but I would not speak to him of it. Marriage? How can I think of it? I have just lost my child and my beloved. Yes, James and I did intend to marry. He gave me this, this token, as a promise to return. He did return to me, but only as his ghost . . . Before he went to sea again we made our plans— but now. Now it is all gone. No, I cannot marry or think of it until I grieve this loss. Henrik needs me. He is enough reason for me to carry on."

"Of course, but is Ola doing all he can, or is he like all the other sailors?" Anna said sarcastically.

Randine stood up abruptly and walked away towards the kitchen with Henrik in her arms, but before Randine could speak, her father put a hand on his wife's arm.

"For the Love of God, Anna, do you always have to provoke a feud? Stop, this minute. Look at what you just said to Randine. For God's sakes apologize Anna! I demand it. Now!"

Randine stopped rocking Henrik for a moment and Anna drew back into her chair. Never before had either of them heard Haagen stand up to her. Randine turned and looked straight at her mother, as she rocked Henrik back and forth.

Anna was so shocked she looked straight at Haagen as if to burn a hole in him, then at Randine, and then back to

Haagen. She turned toward the fire, and swallowed hard.

"I did not mean to suggest, I –I am sorry. It just seems that you could marry first and then go to Laerdal."

"The wedding must be there, in the place of Ola's birth, or in your home church Mother, you know the tradition better than I. There can be no wedding until Ola has more income. At least as a wet nurse I would not be scorned by the church—and the damn Ethics League—who would throw out on the streets an unwed woman with a child." Randine was angry, and she was not going to back down.

"Besides, I will be glad to leave this place. Bergen has been a sorry town for me. Even though I was not born here, but on the way here—isn't that what you said, I was born in a boat in the middle of the fjord?"

"Almost in the boat, we made it to a nearby farm," Mother corrected.

"Let us talk about this later, perhaps over the holiday we can discuss … Perhaps … there is something else we can do…" Father was clearly back to his old ways.

Randine took a deep breath and fussed with Henrik's blanket as she placed him in his cradle, fast asleep. She slowly came back to the fire and sat down with her parents.

"To be honest with you, I do not like the idea of living with a man I do not know. Anyway, I should be at least eighteen to marry. This is the way it is in Laerdal as well as here, is it not? If I am the daughter of a merchant I cannot become pregnant before the betrothal or preferably before the marriage. With a cotter's daughter it is not the same, no one would care, unless I bedded with several men at once. Ola is not James, but he is a good man, and so decent that he wanted to make a plan right away. I was the one who would not discuss it. Now, if you can figure out a better way, you share it with me. Ola would not take money from you for my support. He is not like that. I know that much about him."

"I do not like this one bit Randine, I do not like Ola, and I think he is not a very good man to ask you to do this," Anna said, without a bit of compromise in her voice.

"Mother, it was not his idea, it was Ursula's. She helped me during labor and she helped Ragnild, Ola's betrothed, at birth a few days later. She is the one who suggested it. She brought Henrik to me after his own mother died. Talk to Ursula for a better solution."

"But Randine, you would have to live as Henrik's wet nurse for the rest of your life. Do you really want this?" Anna persisted.

"My God, Mother, this child gives me hope and I give him life. I have lost everything. The least I can do is give him life that my own son could not receive from me because of the ridiculous church rules. Besides, it is your church Ethics Society that takes a dim view of unwed mothers, it is not what I feel is fair. At least I will have dignity going to Laerdal. I detest the way it is, but I cannot change things any more than you. Perhaps if you had found a son that you could love, after Torsten's death, you would have been more cheery all these years."

"Your brother was...." Anna roared now.

Haagen stood up quickly, and stepped between them to grab Anna's hand before striking Randine in the face. "Anna, stop, you will wake the baby!"

Randine kept on speaking to her, but with more caution. "Can you honestly think of another way? It is not about Ola or me. It is about Henrik now. I could not bear for him to be ridiculed for something that was not his fault. He is a blessing to me, to Ola, too, and I am grateful that I do not have to go to another town scorned. Besides it will be an adventure. I am rather looking forward to that. You both well know that I have never been out of Bergen."

Anna was about to start at her again when Haagen faced his wife.

"Anna I think it is time to go. Randine, we would like you to come with the Ericksons and Ursula for Christmas dinner, at least it would seem like family again, I cannot bear the thought not having you there. Will you come?"

"Let me talk to Ursula, I would like to but we shall

see. We would have to bundle up Henrik well," Randine replied. "He should not leave this house, with the Herderers and all."

"Of course, I will send a carriage, and make it a safe, warm journey for you and Henrik. When are we to meet Ola?" Haagen asked, "Will he join us?"

"He leaves for the holidays in Laerdal soon. I will see if there is a good time for you to meet him before he goes. Otherwise, after the season is over, in the New Year," Randine replied.

Anna turned to leave with her husband. She wanted to say something but bit her lip so as not to cause more trouble.

"We will stop again, Randine," Haagen said. "I do not want you going out in the cold with the baby, at least not until Yuletide. We can come for you with the carriage when it is time. We will find a way."

Anna coldly kissed her daughter on the cheek, then Haagen followed with a big hug and a kiss. They took another peek at their adopted grandson. Anna sighed.

"It is not the way I would want it for you Randine, but here he is..."

"Good night Mother, Father, I am glad you came to visit. You know where to find me."

As Anna and Haagen left, Randine turned her baby toward the fire. It seems they would both be facing more heat in the coming days.

Chapter Six
Holiday Return

Christmas Eve, 1820
Dear Diary, How wonderful to see Ralph and Else again. I
have missed them. Do you know who surprised us on Christ-
mas Eve? You won't believe it...

    Lena and Peter had closed the tavern for the Christ-
mas holidays and they were both in a jolly mood. Lena put
more cookies in her basket and Peter hummed a merry
Christmas song as they loaded the carriage and set out to
pick up Randine a few blocks away. The Ericksons' Boarding
House on Valkensdorfsgaten Street, where they also lived,
was just a few blocks from the harbor and a few blocks from
Ursula's house going the opposite direction into town away
from the harbor. The Erickson's humble wooden boarding
house was just large enough for the two of them downstairs, with a large than average dining area near the fireplace and the upstairs rooms for their guests.
    Tonight the walk was too far down too many blocks
in winter, besides the baby needed as much protection
as possible, and Ursula's house was further still off a side
street from Valkensdorfsgaten away from the Stokanes
house overlooking the harbor. After the carriage driver,
Ralph, had picked up Lena and Peter, the horses stopped in
front of Ursula's house. Peter jumped out of the carriage as
it pulled to a stop on the crunching sound of snow. Randine
had just finished nursing Henrik and was bundling up her
sleepy son in a large woolen scarf spread open on the bed.
She wanted to be sure to keep him warm, even the short
distance they would be traveling.
    Randine knew it would be difficult to return to her

parents' home on Nøstertorvet Street. She had not been in the west of Bergen, on that spit of land on the hillside overlooking the water, since she ran away. This u-shaped harbor was what made Bergen such a safe port for ships. The Stokanes house was a large two-story wood-frame structure that spoke her father's status as a merchant. Norway was poor, but Bergen was one of the wealthier cities because of the trade. When she worked for her father she remembered the list of goods he imported; cognac and wine from France, rum from the West Indies, spices and coconut from South America and India and many other goods shipped from all over the world. The German's had established the Hansiatic League decades before from Bergen's port and of course munitions, and other military equipment were also imported and exported. Exports included fish, hides of sheep and goats in the summer and fall as well as barely, some wheat, oats and wool. Randine's father was one of the newly rich from the increase in trade since the struggle for independence had ended with the Danes in 1805. The Erickson's also benefited from more trade in Bergen's busy port, as they could obtain a variety of spirits for the Tavern and more sailors coming in to drink it.

It was the first time Randine had been out of the house since Henrik's birth. It was customary that a newborn not leave the house until six months old, at least until winter had passed, and that the mother only venture out if she had to. There were many folk stories of the child being taken by trolls and Herderers, she-cows that stole babies at night. Randine had made two dolls to put into the bed with them, so the Herderer would be confused if she came to take Henrik. After all, Herderers were not very smart, and everyone knew that. Winter had its own spirits and tales, but Herderers were a danger all year 'round. Such a tiny baby as Henrik, Randine thought, was vulnerable to the Herderers, so she left one doll in the cradle and placed the other doll tucked beside him in his blanket before she carried him out to the carriage.

Peter cleared away the ice on the front steps that led to the street so Randine wouldn't slip when she carried Henrik down to the carriage.

"Hallo my fine young Mother, Randine!" Peter said grinning as he took Randine's arm while he guided her across the snow-covered cobblestones.

"Hello Mr. Erickson, Ralph, good to see you again," Randine said to the driver, as he helped her step into the carriage with Henrik in her arms.

"A good Christmas to you Miss," Ralph answered.

"And to you, Ralph," Randine said kindly. She had always appreciated his quiet service to her family. He had been their driver for as long as she could remember. Peter handed several baskets into the carriage after Randine was settled comfortably into the seat beside Lena. As the last basket was being loaded, they saw a neighbor step out onto her front porch.

"Looks like a fancy feast for the Erickson's tonight!" Mrs. Nester shouted to them from across the street. "What fine table do you sit at tonight Peter Erickson, with such a footman and carriage to take you there?"

Peter turned and looked at Eva Nester and waved merrily, ignoring her comments.

"A good Christmas to you Eva! May you have a warm and happy holiday with or without a carriage!"

Peter was the last to get in, and sat across from the two women facing them chuckling with his small joke.

"That should fix her," he said under his breath.

"That old nosey Eva Nester and her Ethics League, she would love to spread the gossip we abhor," Lena said, patting Randine's hand in reassurance. "Don't mind her, she is just jealous. Though we have never had a Christmas Eve feast with a carriage escort, I would say we are the talk of the neighborhood today. Of course, no one in Norway deserves more than anyone else or there is hell to pay with gossip, that is for sure!"

"I haven't ridden in this carriage for so long. It must have been before I met James, the times when father and I would go to the harbor together. Ralph is such a good man. I remember how the two of them laughed and joked together all the way. Oh, look what is under the seat! Father put the bed warmer here to make the ride warm enough for Henrik!" Randine said sweetly.

The steady clip of the horse's hooves and the hum of the Ralph humming a Christmas tune lulled them into a peaceful silence. As the winter snow dusted the quiet streets, Randine let her senses take in the crispness of air and the stillness of the night, and watched the drifts that made small mounds over and along the streets everywhere.

When they rounded the corner to Nøstertorvet Street, Randine could see the lights in the houses through the carriage window. Mother had placed candles in all the windows. The steam from inside the house from the cooking pots made the lights appear to be glowing orbs.

As they approached her parents' house, Randine's childhood memories clustered around her. There by the tree, she once played with the neighbor children in the snow, rolling snowballs and stacking them for snowball fights. Over there behind the trees, she often played hide-and-seek. There in a neighbor's house she saw herself in the warm kitchen, baking cookies with Martha, her school friend. But most of Randine's memories returned to her times with James.

The carriage came to a stop and Randine felt Ralph climb down and open the carriage door. Her parents' home stood dark with candles in the lamps at either side of the front door. A flurry of snowflakes made this feel like Christmas. Then the large front door opened and out stepped her mother and father in their overcoats to greet them. Father extended his hand to Randine as she stepped out of the carriage, carefully balancing herself with the baby in her arms.

"Welcome daughter, steady now," Haagen said.

"Hello father, good to see you," Randine said, as she stepped down from the carriage and kissed him on the cheek. Then she saw mother with her open arms standing on the steps. She took a deep breath before she ventured up to her mother's waiting embrace. Ralph took her arm after Haagen let go, as he turned to help Lena then Peter out of the carriage.

"Hello Mother, A good Christmas to you!"

"And to you daughter, and to you, little one. Welcome home!" Anna kissed Randine on the cheek. "Bring Henrik in the house before he catches his death."

When she stepped inside the foyer, Randine's eyes widened. She had never seen their house look so beautiful. Candles were lit in every window with fragrant cedar bows around their holders and the fireplace mantel had four large candles with boughs and red ribbons lacing around them. Garlands spiraled up the banister to the second floor. The dining table, visible through the hall in front of them, was set with crystal glasses and painted china plates that her mother had imported from England when Randine was a child. Everything sparkled. There wasn't a thing out of place.

"The house is beautiful mother, it must have taken weeks to decorate."

"We wanted this to be a special Christmas," Anna said quietly.

While the guests handed Anna and Haagen their coats and hats and scarves they hung them on the hooks in the front hall, Randine straightened her simple handspun dress with one hand while she held Henrik with the other and began to move to the couch in the parlor with Lena.

"You and Elsa did a magnificent job. Where did you get the pine boughs?" Randine asked.

"Your father and Ralph got them last week in the woods outside of Bergen. You know the two of them, when they have a scheme."

"Yes, I know. They must have had fun together as usual. Ralph and Elsa, are they dining with us tonight?"

"Oh . . . no, their family from the hills are here visiting them this year. They'll be having a feast of their own tonight—and tomorrow, I might add. After Ralph and his wife serve us, you know, they will be off. The dishes, I am afraid, will be left to us."

"Never mind," Lena reassured her. "This old Norwegian does not like to be waited on anyway. We can all pitch in. I'd feel more comfortable that way."

"Where is Ursula? Did she not come with you?" Anna asked Lena.

"She was called away at the last minute before we arrived. Such is a midwife's life." Anna replied.

"She hopes to be here later." Randine added.

Peter brought in the baskets of food and set them in the hall. The last one he handed to Anna. "A good Christmas to you, Anna, May you have a bright and happy year!" Peter bowed and kissed her hand, as was the custom, while she took the basket in the other.

"Thank you Peter, and to you also," Anna replied as she curtsied slightly. Anna peaked inside the basket to see cookies and a covered bottle with a piece of twine around it.

"Randine, I have your holiday dress upstairs laid out on your bed. Why don't you put it on? You would look much more festive. And of course, you'll want to wear it when we go to church tomorrow."

Randine bristled and did not want to hear the command her mother made, nor her assumption that she would become the dutiful daughter again.

"No, Mother, I am comfortable in this dress. Thank you."

"But it is your bunad, your traditional dress, you must wear it," Anna demanded.

"Anna, let us not discuss this now," Haagen said, entering the room "We are about to have some Akavit. Let us be glad and celebrate the season." Haagen unwrapped the basket to see inside. "What did they bring to us this fine evening? Cookies—and how wonderful, pickled herring!"

Lena stood between Anna and Randine, and escorted Anna into the living room where Peter was waiting with an empty glass.

"Come now dear, let us celebrate the season. Perhaps a toast, Peter we need a toast, yes, or Haagen, please a toast to begin our celebration together," Lena said.

Anna stood confused and angry, and then she was handed a glass with some Akavit.

"To Randine and Henrik, let us celebrate the child and such helpful friends, the Erickson's!" Haagen said with exuberance.

"To Haagen and Anna, for their fine feasting!" Peter added. Anna managed a smile, and bowed slightly to acknowledge the toast.

Randine lifted her glass and nodded, while looking down at little Henrik, wiggling against her shoulder. She hoped this wasn't going to be a holiday that disappointed her mother's expectations, like so many of them had in the past. At least the drink would pacify her for a while.

The scent of roasted pork and potatoes came wafting in from the kitchen as Elsa opened the door and came in to place cookies and treats on a table along the wall beside the couch.

"Miss Randine! Oh, Miss Randine we have missed you so!" Elsa could not restrain herself. She set down the platter of cookies and ran to her with open arms. She hugged Randine around her neck, and then took a peek at baby James in her arms embracing both of them.

"Oh, what a bundle of joy you have here! Is he not a wonder?"

"Elsa, meet Henrik, my new son," Randine said proudly.

"Oh isn't he a bundle of love. What a fine boy!" Elsa gushed. "Your Mama and Papa must be so proud."

Randine did not answer, but glanced at Lena, who smiled reassuringly.

"How wonderful you look! A grown up lady!" Elsa said. "And you dear, how are you on your own?"

As usual Elsa bluntly stated that which was supposed to be kept under the rug.

"Thank you Elsa, I feel very good, Ursula has helped me so much." Randine said clearly. "And you, how have you been?"

"Elsa, aren't there more cookies and pastries?" Anna said sharply.

"Yes, 'Ma'am, there surely are. I will bring them right away." Turning to Randine, she winked and whispered, "I'll be talking to you later, Miss." She whispered so loudly that everyone could hear it. Elsa hurried into the kitchen with her usual quick arthritic shuffle.

"It is good to see her Mother. Their children are well?" Randine asked to break her mother's tension on the bunad question. "Yes, for now they have the four children. The children help us, too, from time to time. It gives the family work," Mother said, with her air of authority. "Her sons helped Ralph and I gather the pine boughs. We had a wonderful time," Haagen said with a grin, ignoring his wife's foul mood.

"Did I ever tell you about the time when my brother Ender and I were hunting in the Mountains?" Haagen began his story. "We came around a large fir tree, near a birch grove. We both had on our snowshoes, as the snow was deep up there, I tell you. Then suddenly Ender heard an odd bellowing sound. It was a moose howl, sure as I am standing here. The moose came in sight and she was not further away than here to that kitchen door. I could swear to you the moose was forty hands high, it was bigger than any troll, I can tell you, bellowing at us! OHoooo! Then we saw it behind us, a young one. I grabbed Ender, "Run!" I said, without a moment to waste. Just as we lopped off in our clumsy snowshoes, there goes the little one right to his mother. Well we didn't stop until we reached the trail that led us there. We dared not look back, as that mother moose would surely call in her kin, I can tell you!!"

Everyone laughed at the sight of the two brothers being chased by the huge moose. Peter was about to add his embellishments, when he was interrupted by a knock on the door, and everyone shifted attention from Peter's new story.

"Who could that be? Ah, it must be Ursula," Anna said impatiently. "There are no more guests invited."

"It is the holiday, someone visiting no doubt. Excuse me Lena, hold that story Peter, I shall get the door."

Haagen put down his glass and walked briskly to the front door. When he opened it, he saw a very tall man that he did not recognize wearing a red cap. Haagen noticed the government issued wool coat that was the mark of any sailor. Underneath the coat the man was wearing his dress uniform.

"Good holiday to you, sir! I am Ola Tomasson Lysne. I believe this is the childhood home also of your daughter Randine Hakonshatter Stokanes Luster?"

Haagen stood there, shocked to see him.

"Why, yes, yes, you are Henrik's... Yes. Come in," Haagen stuttered. "Randine, could you come here, please!"

When she heard her father ask her to come to the door, Randine could not imagine who it might be. She handed the baby to Lena, and walked to the door as Ola stepped over the threshold into the foyer.

"Ola! How could you be here?! I thought you would be in Laerdal..." He bowed to her from the waist, and she stepped towards him, and curtsied in return.

"Merry Christmas, Randine." Ola smiled at her.

"Merry Christmas, Ola." Randine said her voice betraying her nervousness.

"It...it's Ola!" Lena stuttered.

"Ola?" Peter repeated then under his breath. "What a brave man he is to come here!"

Anna was flustered with the news, and could not take it in at first. Then she turned on her heels and went straight for the door. When she saw this tall stranger standing next to her daughter, her heart melted when she saw how respectful he was toward Randine. Anna stood there for a moment, watching as the Erickson's greeted him.

Tears of joy ran down Randine's cheeks, as she saw the Erickson's extend their hands to him, and he turned to introduce himself to Randine's parents.

"Yes, we have just met," Haagen winked at him, which disarmed Ola temporarily. Ola extended his long-fingered hand out to Haagen and the two men shook hands heartily.

Then he turned to Anna. Randine led him to Anna for his protection.

"Mother this is Ola Tomasson Lysne from Laerdal."

"Good Christmas to you Heir Strondi Stokanes," Ola said politely, bowing at the waist to kiss her hand as she extended it to him.

"Good Christmas to you, too, Mr. Lysne. You are brave to come here," Anna said admiringly, but with her usual curtness.

"I thought you should meet the culprit," Ola said with a chuckle. "Since Randine is taking such good care of my son Henrik, Randine is a part of my family now as Henrik's … well as his mother was."

No one spoke, but Peter laughed at his bold statement. "Come have some Akavit, Heir Culprit, Ola. Come in, I was about to tell another story."

Haagen took Ola's coat, hat, and scarf and hung them on an empty hook in the hall. Ola's uniform was dark blue with brass buttons and a white buckle that set off the waist of his coat. He looked as sharp as he could, clean shaven, with a long gait as he strode into the parlor. Ola was so tall he had to duck his head slightly under the archway into the parlor so as not to hit his head on the transom.

Randine was still in shock, and took Henrik from Lena then laced her arm through her father's. Anna sat on the coach staring into her drink. She did not know what to say to him. She could not help but like Ola. He disarmed her. She stared off into space. Peter resumed his storytelling, as if there was not a shock still hovering in the room. Somewhere in Peter's prattling on about his adventures hunting on the far range with his brother, Anna lost her bitterness as she looked at the unexpected scene. Ola had to be from a good family if he showed himself this way.

Elsa came in from the kitchen, and she saw the tall sailor towering above everyone else.

"Elsa, I want you to meet Løytnant Ola Tomasson Lysne, from Laerdal. He is the father of Henrik," Randine whispered over the story that was underway.

Else wiped her hands on her apron to shake his hand.

"Gooden naught, Løytnant Lysne, Gooden naught," Elsa said, bowing from the waist.

"Good Christmas Eve to you, ma'am," Ola replied bowing slightly.

Then Elsa said, "We all love Randine so, in this house." She meant the help, but Ola took it as the entire household, including the family.

"Yes," Ola whispered as loudly, "I can see that." Ola looked down at Randine with a grin.

"You make a fine pair," Elsa said with her usual abandon. "A fine pair."

"Will you add another place at the table Elsa? Ola will be staying for dinner, won't you Ola?" Randine pleaded.

"If you will have me, yes. It would be my pleasure."

"What say you Mother? Can Ola stay?" Randine demurred to her mother who was listening to the conversation.

"Of course," Anna said with surrender in her voice and a wave of her hand.

Elsa raced off again, always at a trot, it seemed. When Peter finished his story the three men laughed at the punch line. Though Ola missed most of the story from his introduction to Else.

After the story had ended everyone found a place to sit down in the living room as Peter directed the conversation, in his usual master-of-ceremonies style: "So Løytnant

Ola, tell us what kept you from going to Laerdal this holiday. All of the men go home if they can, don't they?"

"Well," Ola began, "Our boat got turned around with the storm that hit the north coast two days ago. I realized I was being turned around for a good reason. Our captain gave us this night and tomorrow night off, with only a skeleton crew to watch, as the storms were so bad, there are few who could brave the seas anyway. I felt it was important for me to meet Randine's parents, so I thought to come here and surprise … everyone." Ola dipped his head and looked around the room.

"Yes, and that you have, I might add!" Haagen chuckled. "We are glad you have come. You must be from a fine family to show up, I admire this of you young man."

"I knew of your brother and your father, Løytnant Lysne," Anna said. "You are from Laerdal. I am from Årdal. Haagen and I were married there, too. The two villages and Sogndal had summer harvest festivals together. I believe we may have met your brother once."

"What a small country we live in. Do you miss your home?" Ola asked.

"Sometimes, then at times, not," Anna answered. "There is nothing like the country for me. Though I do love the refinement of city life," as she lifted her crystal glass.

"I wish I could take Randine there. You know we celebrate the Christmas holiday for weeks," Ola said, expressing love of his farm country, though Anna took it as a comparison.

"Yes, I remember it well. At least in the city we do not have to see all the slaughtering and blood on the farm beforehand in November," she said with a pinch in her voice.

"I have never had a holiday away from Laerdal to know the difference in the city. Somehow I have always managed to make it home every year. But I look forward to this Christmas here in Bergen," Ola said, drawing closer to Randine.

"A first Christmas with my—no—our son."

Just then Elsa came out of the kitchen door. "Dinner is ready, it is on the table. Please come."

Peter and Haagen waited for their wives to rise from their seats, and offered their arms to escort them to the table. Ola and Randine stepped aside graciously to honor their elders. The three couples, with Henrik in Randine's arm, walked through the front hall and into the dining room, where the fire blazed in the hearth. The table was arrayed with the Christmas ham, hot and juicy, adorned with spiced apples and sprigs of pine around the platter. Lefsa, potato pancakes, piled high on a large plate beside a large bowl of lutefisk, boiled cod, that had been soaked in lye for days, then washed clean, boiled and served with butter. Then there was a bowl of rømmegrøt or sour cream soup and mashed rutabagas in a cream sauce. Warm hot buns, wrapped in a cloth, rested in a basket near the center of the table. Candles glowed in silver candelabras imported from England through Haagen's import/export company.

"Elsa and Mother you have out done yourselves," Randine said with appreciation.

"Oh, the table looks splendid. How fine a meal we will share tonight!" Peter said rubbing his belly.

After everyone sat down at the dining table, Haagen gave thanks for the meal, and for his daughter, and for Ola, who had come out of the cold into the warmth of the family hearth. He gave thanks for his new grandson Henrik, who was nestled in his mother's embrace. He gave thanks for the Ericksons who were part of the family now that they had taken care of Randine in her hour of need. And he gave thanks for his wife, for whom he asked a special blessing. Then he remembered the Christ child in the manger, and Mary and Joseph. He gave thanks for the eve of the birth of the Christ. Then he lifted his Christmas stein, and asked for a toast.

"To our blessed child, who has come home with her adopted son, Henrik, and his father, Ola. They are like Mary and Joseph tonight, here in our house. May our home be the Bethlehem where they found shelter. May their life be long and blessed."

Anna looked up at Haagen and gave him a riveting glare. Peter and Lena toasted his prayer. At first Randine was as shocked as her mother at the analogy with Jesus and Joseph and Mary, but as she thought about it, she felt pleased. It was her father's way to stop her mother from any more negative talk, at least until dinner was over. Randine realized it was a beautiful prayer. She took hold of father's hand and gave it a squeeze. He brought her hand up to his lips and kissed it.

"I love you Papa," Randine whispered.

After dinner the men went into the parlor to talk, smoke, and drink more Akavit. Lena and Anna took to the dishes. Randine nursed Henrik in the dining room near the hearth. His bright eyes looked up at her, as though he sensed her peace and contentment with her family. It was then that Henrik smiled his first smile. Randine's thoughts spun as she noticed how much he looked like his father, 'Ola is a good man, I could like him at least.'

Through the clacking of the dishes, she could faintly hear Lena and her mother speaking together in the kitchen. She could not hear what the men were saying through the glass doors, but she could tell who was speaking by the pitch of their voices. Ola had a deep voice, and was slow and methodical in his speech. Peter always sounded as though he was up to some mischief, with laughter in his voice. Father's voice was commanding at times, yet timid when he offered his opinion or made a suggestion. His voice was neither deep nor bold, but always trying to please and make the best of a situation.

"Young man, you know I could use some help at the docks. Of course, it would have to be when you are done with your post in the military. But I would like to offer you a position with me if you want it," Haagen said.

"Thank you sir, but I am a farmer at heart, and a sailor by necessity, though I love the sea. Since I cannot till my elder brother's farm as he inherited everything as is usual in Norway, and there is no land for me as a second son, I will be staying in the military until I am transferred to Laerdal as part of the Army, then I might even be stationed in Laerdal, with trips up and down the fjord. I will have ten years in the service in another year, then I will be eligible for a promotion and my pension, it will be assured in another ten at a higher rate than I am getting now. That is my plan."

"It sounds like a good one," Peter said loudly to show his approval. "Yes, you will have your pension, and be able then to farm while you live in your home town. Sounds like as good a plan as any I have heard. Most sailors have no vision at all, just the next port, if you know what I mean."

"And what are your intentions with my daughter?" Haagen sounded stern, but wanted to make himself clear.

"Until I make the raise, I cannot ask for her hand, though it is in my mind to marry her, of course, eventually. She is just fifteen so we will have to wait until she is of age, and we can save money for a wedding. She can live in Bergen until the baby is old enough to travel. My plan is to move to Laerdal with Randine, but she will not speak to me of any plans just now. I know she is still adjusting to the shock of losing her man and her own son. If she comes to Laerdal as a wet nurse to Henrik, there can be no doubt in any minds that she is a good and decent woman. Then she can make her place there, and perhaps by then... Well, she will have to tell you any more than that as she will not discuss plans at this time. My mother could always use an extra pair of hands, as she is growing older now, and my brother is always glad to see me during harvest season."

"She would go as the wet nurse to Henrik. My daughter has said this much. I know how the farming areas are, especially with landowner's sons. They must uphold the righteousness of the church for all the other families according to the piety of the church fathers. I hear it has become more conservative there of late," Haagen replied.

"Yes, the new vicar in Laerdal is very stern. He is making it difficult for everyone who has bundled on winter nights. Many of the cotters have children born before their weddings. It is more common than not in the country. But I ask you, how can a young couple hold a wedding feast and gather the families when they are still finding work and trying to scrape together the barest of needs?" Ola complained. "Most cannot afford to carve a spoon, let alone hold the wedding of their ancestors. There is no place for young couples to know each other before they wed, except through night-courting."

"Yes, I see, if Randine is the wet nurse, she can be there without scrutiny. She can have the baby nearby, and see you on leave, and wait until you are ready to buy or rent a cabin of your own," Haagen said thoughtfully.

"And there will be no bundling until the wedding," Randine said flatly with a grin on her face. She had put Henrik in the cradle her mother had set beside the fireplace in the dining room. All the men felt her intrusion as it was not the place of a woman to intrude on men's conversations after dinner. Yet her intention was to make herself clear. She burst out laughing at the sight of the dumbfounded men. And they all began to laugh.

"Well, daughter, is your son asleep? Did you overhear us?" Haagen said with some compromise in his voice.

"Yes, father, I heard. He is in the cradle by the fire in the dining room. I want to make it plain that I have not been able to think about any arrangement of going to Laerdal as the wet nurse or maid. It would be nice if you consulted me about plans you are making about my life. But I have to admit, what choices are there for a woman?"

Ola was surprised by her boldness, but Randine thought he should know the sort of woman he was dealing with, and she was not going to just go along because the men planned it to be so.

"Now, now, we all want the best for you my dear. Your commitment will be plain enough, Randine, for you to go there if you choose to. Ola's will be made when he brings you to his home. Perhaps you two will not have to wait until so long for a wedding," Peter cajoled.

"That is not up to me," Randine said softly. "Time will tell. Besides, I have some midwife work I can do here with Ursula for the time being."

"Work with Ursula?" Peter interjected.

"Yes, I am to be her assistant cleaning and scrubbing the items she uses, and as soon as I can, I hope to do more," Randine smiled.

"Yes, well, actions do speak louder. Let's all have another round." Peter lifted the bottle to pour them some cognac as they had finished the Akavit. "This is the best of my tavern, all the way from France. I believe the shipment came through your merchant services Haagen!" Peter chuckled, and Haagen clicked his glass.

"There are advantages to being in the import business, and this is one of them," Haagen stated with a grin as he sipped his cognac.

"Excuse us, won't you, I only have a few more moments until I need to be back on the ship," Ola said, bowing low to the men as he took Randine's arm and escorted her back to the chairs at the dining room hearth. As she closed the French doors to the dining room, they sat down near the fire and cradle, Ola folded his hands and sighed.

"I know what you say is true Randine. But I cannot be my own man unless I make my own way. I must find a way to make a living without my brother. I love my brother, he has been a father to me since our father died when I was just a boy. But you must know, this desire is for the good of both of us. I want to support my own wife. I cannot do this until I can transfer, until I can earn enough to save for a cabin of our own. Do you see? Betrothal is out of the question until I have been promoted. Then...we shall see."

Randine gazed into the fire while he spoke, and did not reply at first, but then she said: "Ola, I wish I could just fall in love with you. It would make everything between us easier. I wish—well it doesn't matter what I wish. A woman has so little choice in her life, once she has a child."

"I cannot ask you to marry me until I am a man with my own property to offer you."

"I am in no hurry to go to Laerdal, nor to marry anyone. Ursula has offered that I train with her to be a midwife. After I have spent enough time training with her, I can be a midwife on my own. Then perhaps, I can go to Laerdal with a profession to support me, as well as with our son, your son."

"You are feeding him Randine. He is as much yours now, as he is mine. I would have lost both my love and my son if it was not for you." Ola could not help himself. He took her hand, and kissed it. Randine drew back out of surprise but only slightly. The two of them sat by the fire for a long time in silence. Ola moved his chair closer to Randine and took the sleeping Henrik in his arms. The baby nestled into his chest and Ola smiled at the knowledge that his scent was a comfort to his son. Then he reached in his pocket with his other hand and drew out a carved little soldier for his son.

"I made this for him." Ola said. "Merry Christmas, Henrik." He reached in again and brought out a betrothal spoon, carved with mountain flowers around the bowl.

"This is for you Randine, but I won't give it to you now. I will keep it, as a promise until it is time for us to discuss more of a plan together, when you are ready."

Randine teared up and then placed her hand on his gently as he held the spoon. Ola put it back in his pocket.

They could hear Anna and Lena stirring in the parlor with the men. Her father drew closed the doors to the parlor so they would not disturb Randine and Ola. For that moment at least, with Henrik asleep in his father's arms, they were a small family... Randine knew then that their losses were deep and had to heal before they could consider each other. He had as much grief as Randine did. She could see that now.

"Perhaps we can write to each other. That way we could get to know each other first," Randine suggested. "We have just met a month ago. Time can be a friend to both of us."

Ola smiled at her cautiously and sighed, "Yes, we will find our way, if the fates allow. Randine, I am so grateful to you, you have been a Godsend to me and Henrik." He handed Henrik back to his new mother. "Thank you for everything. You saved me from your torment of a double loss. Two in one awful moment."

Randine could not speak, but looked up at Ola with tears in her eyes and touched Ola's hand. He cautiously ventured to place an awkward arm around Randine and Henrik.

Chapter Seven
Ola at Sea

Saturday, 20 January 1821
Dear Diary, Ola leaves today. Who knows when Henrik will
see him again. May he have safe travels... I do wish him well.

Ola was able to extend his leave for the holiday season, and go to his homeland of Laerdal after the New Year
when the storms subsided. It was so good to be home for
at least some time. He and a mate from Laerdal rowed the
150-mile journey back and forth from Bergen. It took them
a few days each way.

Upon his return to Bergen, he said his good-byes to
Randine, Henrik and Ursula and within the week his captain
and crew were stocked and ready to leave port by the tall
ship they were to sail after the holidays.

They made it to the other side of Norway around the
end of the spoon, as some of the men liked to say, and sailed
on to Christiania where they dropped off sheepskins and
barley from nearby farmer's harvests. The sailors gathered
stores for the longer voyage they would make to Haarlem,
Netherlands. The ship rounded the harbor on its way from
Copenhagen as Ola and his mates headed north up the Kat-
tegat, past Alborg in Denmark towards the mouth of the
Skagerrak straights to head southwest out to the North Sea.
There were no reports of storms from the incoming ships,
so they were assured of a good sail from Copenhagen, and
set their course south, as the captain ordered, towards the
Netherlands. They had a shipment of arms and grain from
Copenhagen to unload at the port of Haarlem. There was
not much trouble these days, now that the British and the
Russians had made peace.

Ola loved the feeling of setting sail again away from

port, as they made several tacks out the Skagerrak straits between Norway and Denmark. This zigzag course allowed them to gain the most of the wind as they sailed out to sea.

"Say good bye to the homeland for a time mates," the captain shouted from the wheel. "It's the last you'll see Norway for a few months."

As the men curled line into coils or tightened down halyards that were knocking in the wind, several looked over the rail toward the last view of the rugged Norwegian coastline.

Ola felt a tug in his heart, as it was always hard for him to leave Norway. Now that he had a son, and it made it harder. Ola watched the coast disappear behind them as the captain made his last tack, ordered sails set to the south-west, and they zigzagged out into the open sea.

Ola would miss Copenhagen too, as he remembered his lover Lisa again. He soon discovered Lisa to be more fickle than he had imagined, as she had already met someone new and could not wait for Ola to make up my mind. Still there were plenty of women to bed with this time. Plenty who could be bought for a skilling or two. Though Ola did think of Randine now and again. It was different for him with the women this time. He did not want to bed, he just wanted to have a drink and enjoy their company. Was Randine affecting him already? Ola wasn't sure.

Ola's drifting thoughts were snapped back into the moment by the Captain as he shouted again for Ola to hoist the topsails, as the wind was steady and keen. After they saluted, he and his shipmates scurried up the mast and the ratlines to the sheets midway. A small platform gave them enough footing to snap the lines free and set the sail to fill with the blast of wind that set their speed a few knots higher.

Ola glanced down at the Captain, and was nodded an approving glance. They were lucky to have such a good Captain. He did love the men, though he was as stern as a Captain should be. For many of young men he was like a father when on board ship.

Ola took a moment to look across the expanse of the wild North Sea. They had only Denmark in sight as they pulled away from the last sight of land. This was the life Ola loved, setting sail into the unknown. Though he had crossed the North Sea many times he never tired of the adventure of it. He forgot about farming out here, and was quite happy leaning into the wind. Though this time, his safety was more of a factor, as he wanted to be with Henrik.

This trip they would head out further east towards England, but not as far as to see the coast. The straightest course was to the south. A northwesterly wind seemed to be picking up and they lost sight of land altogether as the wind pushed their square-rigger on the course east/south-east heading for the Netherlands.

The run down the coast was easy enough, without tacking at all they thought that they could make Haarlem by the morning if the wind didn't slack off. As the skeleton shift took the helm from the Captain, Ola and his mates went below for supper. It would be a long night for some. They knew they might as well rest while they could. They would be on four-hour shifts through the night. Ola was to be on at midnight. He had supper then rested in his berth. Midnight to 4 a.m. was the hardest shift, as they could not see a thing and only had the stars and the moon to guide them. The moon would be out tonight if the clouds did not roll in.

By midnight the wind had grown wild. His mate Halver had brought in the topsails, and the crew shortened even the main, with the help of his friend Rolf. Ola was awake before his shift, as the commotion on deck was hard to sleep through. As he poked his head out the hatch, the rain pelted the deck.

"Best get your oils skins on man," the Captain passed the word.

" 'Tis a big blow out there mate." Ola's buddy Rolf had slapped Ola's shoulder as he passed him on his way to the bunk. Rolf was soaked through.

"Right, sounds like it from the howls in the rigging," Ola said to Rolf. He followed Rolf to his bunk and reached for a scarf to wrap around his neck, and a second cap for his head, as he slid into his oil-skinned gear to protect him from the wind and icy rain.

"Looks like a long night," Rolf said as he closed his eyes.

"All hands, All hands!!" The captain shouted, as another mate rang the bell that called them all on deck.

"Shit, man, I just came from ratlines!" Rolf complained as his head had just rested on the pillow.

Ola pulled on his oilskins over his wool clothes as he scurried away from Rolf to get to the hatch. "Come on man, we'll get through this one together." Ola slapped his friend on the foot as he pulled himself up the ladder to the deck.

As Ola stuck his head through the hatch, the wind was tossing the sails and the sheets back and forth wildly. The captain had just ordered the mainsail down, as they would be riding this one out without sail.

Ola tightened his hood and jammed on his gloves as he raced up the lines towards the mainsail, the ship tossed them right and left. He could barely hang on, as he reached the base of the mast. The wind was so strong everything on deck had been tied down with extra lines. Ola grabbed extra lashes and laid them around his neck to take the mainsail boom vertical and tie it to the main, once he scrambled up the mast.

"We'll lose our sails if we don't secure them!" Rolf shouted.

This would be tricky. Ola climbed up the mast on the ratlines that laced up it. He tugged on the lines around his neck and to be sure they were still there. He could see the feet and backside of two of his mates on the same platform above the deck he had been standing on hours earlier watching the sunset over Denmark. They were hours out to sea now, and the North Sea was earning its reputation as the most deadly sea in Europe. Tonight was to be a test of survival.

Ola was bigger and heavier than most of the men, so his size gave him an advantage when it came to the rigging, he could scramble up and down, without fear of being blown off the mast. This had happened with smaller men. Still he tied a safety line around himself just in case.

When he reached the platform again, he shouted to his mates.

"I'll grab this end of the sail, while you two get the other end." The three of them eased out on the opposite sides of the boom and began to tuck the wild sail into it self as best they could. Just as they were lashing it down, a huge wave broke over the bow.

"Hang on!" Ola shouted.

The crash on deck felt like a giant fist had been slapped onto the deck. Ola grabbed one of his mates by the waist smashing him to the mast like a sandwich.

"Hold on!" Ola commanded.

"I can't, I can't...my hands are...frozen!" Harrold shouted.

"Put them in your pants, and I'll hold on for both of us!" Ola shouted back.

Ola was so large that he covered Harrold completely when he wrapped his arms around him to hold on to the mast. The third mate, Lars, had managed to finish lashing the sail to the boom and secured it. Now they had to get the boom parallel to the mast before they could go below and ride the storm out. Lars came to the mast and held on to Harrold. Ola knew what he would do. Grabbing Harrold and securing another line to him, he shouted in Lars' ear.

"Ok mate, here's what we're doing. I'll secure this end of the boom to the mast. Wait till the next wave, then after I drop Harrold to the deck, grab the boom and secure it on the other end."

Lars nodded. Ola tied a rope around Harrold's arms and chest. Then Ola saw the wave break, as he grabbed the mast again. Ola could hear shouts below but could not hear what the Captain said.

Another wave crashed over the deck and some of the

cargo on deck broke loose. It was plain to see they were all in trouble now below. More mates scurried around trying to lash barrels down, as they rolled from side to side. Ola could see that they were caught in a gale. Ola, Harrold and Lars could not go down, and they couldn't go up either. Harrold was almost delirious from cold and Ola knew he had to get him below as soon as possible. But the chaos on deck was preventing him from lowering him down.

Ola turned Harrold around until they were nose to nose. "Harrold, man, you have to stay with us. Look, as soon as they are secure down there, I will lower you down. Just hold on man. Hold on."

Harrold focused on Ola and tried to nod. Then Ola could see blood trickling down Harrold's face. He had hit his head somehow with the last wave. He had a big gash on his head. He was almost unconscious. Just then another wave broke, this time some of the men on deck were washed to the side.

"Man overboard! Man Overboard!" One man shouted.

Ola knew all he could do was hold on. The boom they tried to lash was thrashing around. Lars gave a huge tug and the boom pivoted into a vertical position. Ola lashed Harrold to the mast while he reached below the catwalk to lash the other end of the boom to the mast.

Then he signaled to Lars to help him with Harrold. Lars scurried down the mast, and held on to the mast as another wave broke across the deck over him.

"He hit his head . . . his hands are frozen—we have to get him below!" Ola shouted to Lars. Harrold was unconscious.

"We're better off here, look at the waves! We could never make it below decks."

"If we time it right, if we can just land on the deck, we might be able to scuttle down the forward hatch. Forget about the reaching the aft cabin."

Lars looked below at the cargo lines that were beating the deck. The forward hatch was just before the mast. If they moved fast enough they might just make it. At least some of them might. If not, they would take on water, a lot of water, in the hold.

"You free the hatch in the back, make it like a hinge, open up the hatch door towards the mast. When you are inside, tighten it down and wait for the next wave. After the wave washes over, I'll lower Harrold down to the top of the deck, you grab his legs and pull him below. Wait 'til you hear him land on the hatch. Then we repeat with each one of us. I'll pound twice and follow him down. But wait 'till you hear me pound."

"Ok, mate, sounds like it will work. It is our best hope." Just then a wave broke over the deck and the three of them huddled together grabbing the mast. As the water cleared the deck, Ola shouted. "Now!"

Lars let go and scurried down the ratlines as fast as he could. He could see another wave coming, so he grabbed the mast and held on. The boat pitched and the boards of the deck seemed to moan under the strain. The icy wave hit Lars hard. He looked up and all he could see was water. Then the deck cleared, and he knew this was his chance. He loosened the line from the hatch and pried it up. He timed it just right to scurry down and slam the hatch shut before the next wave hit. He held onto the handle inside the hatch and hung his whole weight on it, as he could hear the next wave break. His mates were below some were sick from the tossing. Others had made their way to the forward hatch.

"Harrold is hurt. Ola has him on the mast. Help me mates, we need to get him in on the next wave!" Lars shouted to the other men below.

Ola waited until he could see there would be a lull between breakers. Then he dropped Harrold to the deck as he landed on the hatch crumpling below the mast. Two mates below pushed up the hatch and pushed aside the weight of Harrold's body. They saw his head and crumpled body at the base of the mast.

"Grab him!" Lars shouted.

Someone grabbed his oilskins and sweater and
pulled him below head first as they heard Ola shout above.
Harrold slid in and the man who was last on the handle
slammed the hatch closed with the sea washing in after him
only slightly. They got it closed just in time.

They could hear the next breaker pound the deck
like a thousand hammers. Lars passed Harrold to the men
below and they carried him to his bunk wrapping him in
blankets and put his hands in a bowl of cold water. Then he
waited for Ola's knock on the hatch.

Ola was tied to the mast and couldn't get free. He got
a spike from his waistband, and tried to pry the knot loose.
Every time he tried, another wave crashed and he had to
grab the mast again. Slowly he got the line loosened. But ice
was forming on everything, and he was sure this was the
worst storm he had ever seen. As he was getting the last of
the lines unknotted, a huge wave crashed over the deck, and
he was sure he would be lost. He grabbed the mast and held
on for dear life. He was up the mast at the first platform.
That is how high the seas were over the deck!

The wave washed over him and in those seconds of
icy sea waves he started to pray.

"Lord if you get me out of this, I swear, I'll do whatever you want. Help me please."

As Ola finished speaking, the wind seemed to die
down just a bit. He looked up and the storm edge could be
seen above him. Stars were breaking through the layers of
sleet. One cloud parted and uncovered the moon, shining
a beam of silver across the turbulent sea. He could see the
face of someone smiling at him. It was a woman, perhaps
Freya or Mother Mary. Then he felt touched by the moon as
the clouds swallowed it again.

The sea was still tossing the ship back and forth, but
he could see a shooting star right through the hole where
the moon just slipped out of sight. Ola knew it was an answer to his prayer.

When he looked at the knot again he was able to free

himself. He secured the boom well enough. He slid down the mast and slapped hard on the hatch. Lars opened the hatch, and Ola scrambled in grabbing the handle on the hatch, latching the hatch with the hook from the inside. Ola was soaked through from the last icy wave, but he was safe below decks.

"The storm is breaking mates. I just saw the moon!" Ola declared.

A cry of joy came out of the men, and Ola fell into his bunk. He was dazed by the moon. What was that? Who was that face in the moon? He still saw the mysterious face when he closed his eyes.

"How's Harrold?" Ola asked Lars.

"He's resting, has a bad gash. His hands are on ice to thaw them. But he will make it," Lars replied. "How are you?"

Ola didn't reply, but looked at Lars through his fingers placed over his face. His look told Lars what he already knew. That was a rough one.

The wind seemed to subside, as Ola and the other men were left to rest while the Captain and his first mate worked above to set their course and tie down the last of the barrels. All the mates that washed overboard had lifelines on, so they were recovered, though a bit worse for wear. At least they did not lose any of the men. Ola rolled over and wrote a few lines in his journal.

Sunday, 21 January 1821

> *A face in the moon touched me*
> > *in the storm.*
> > *How sweet the smile,*
> > *how long the touch of light.*

Ola rolled towards the wall on his bunk and soon began to drift off. His thoughts stirred as he fell asleep. Who touched me? Was it the moon? No. It was a woman's touch.

He remembered Randine's smile. Was she smiling at him through the moon? No it could not be or was that the Virgin Mary, or the moon itself? He could not tell. But he knew there was a message, and his prayer to help him in his moment of need had been answered.

He dreamt he could see that face again. This time in the sky above Laerdal, this time, it was Randine. He was walking with her out of the church after their wedding. She had a necklace on. It was one he had never seen before. On a gold chain, a pendant hung—a wave caught in circle of gold, like the moon. When Ola awoke, he knew his destiny was to be with Randine. Somehow their union was destined and blessed by the Gods. This he will do for the love he knew was possible, for his gratitude for Henrik being alive and for his life being saved in the storm. No more women in port. Perhaps that is the message more than anything. He hadn't caught anything yet. Thank God. Now he had a reason to stay clean.

Chapter Eight
The Apprentice

Friday, 30 March 1821
Dear Diary, I am so excited to begin washing dirty sheets for
Ursula, I have work! Perhaps I can earn my way after all!

Ursula welcomed Randine as her assistant. Her duties included washing and cleaning the birth stool and the pig bladder used for an enema as well as sheets and towels and nightgowns used for birthing. Randine had not worked this hard even for Lena and she loved supporting Ursula who took care of so many.

She was glad Ola was away as it took the pressure off having to make up her mind. She loved her independence and the adventure of attending to the women in need. Randine told Ola in a recent letter that his support was helpful, and that her midwife work with Ursula was being saved for Henrik's future.

Randine prayed for Ola often. She heard from the port master and in a brief letter from Ola that his orders had changed and was now sailing somewhere near Haarlem and would be gone for most of the month. They had come through a terrible storm. But he did not give her any details about it except to share a poem with her about the moon, which she found beautiful and mysterious. She wondered if he thought about her at all.

This summer he would make it back to Laerdal by land from Christiana once they were docked on the other side of Norway. It was several days hiking from Christiana to Laerdal. He would not be able to come to Bergen as he would be making the same return across country back to Christiana from Laerdal. This meant that they would have to wait another year or more to go to Laerdal. She was disappointed it would take another year, but glad she had work and Henrik to keep her busy.

Ursula's home, though tiny, had enough room for Henrik and Randine as they slept in the loft above the dining area off the kitchen. They didn't need much room. She was so often attending the needs of Ursula's work in the kitchen and cooking for others.

Henrik loved being surrounded by the attention of his mother and a grandmother such as Ursula. He was six months old now and able to crawl around and coo.

Randine also took him for a walk in a tram her parents had bought for her. There were children near by when they walked to the same park, Nylirdstangen near Lungegdrdsvatnet Lake. There were geese and ducks and tiny sailboats that grandfathers and their grandsons sailed back and forth. Some made boats of leaves or sticks. Others had made boats of wooden planks, exact replicas of boats in the harbor. That spring, an early thaw had made the water on the pond possible to sail earlier than ever. Everyone knew it would freeze again, but it was fun to see summer activities so soon in the park. Henrik pointed to the ducks and boats as Randine strolled him around the lake before returning back to the house.

After she had been home and banked the fire, putting Henrik down for a nap, Minister Larstrom came to the door of Ursula's house with Haagen Stokanes. Randine answered it and was surprised to see him there with her father. She did not invite them in, as they were visiting many families who lost relatives and this was one stop of many.

"Miss Stokanes, tomorrow we are burying the corpses of those who died in the winter as the ground has now thawed enough. There will be a burial for Ola's betrothed, Ragnild. It would be a Christian burial. Would you Randine want to be there in Ola's absence, representing the family since Ragnild was Henrik's real mother? Her parents are from another district, and cannot be present, as they have other children."

"If you are presiding over a funeral or any service, I will not attend." Randine told the minister flatly. "Henrik's real mother? Indeed! I am his real mother now."

"Randine!" He father shouted. Her father was upset with her. But could anyone anticipate a different reaction from a young woman scorned by the same man? Haagen wondered. Secretly he was proud of her.

"Father, you of all people know how I feel about the church, his church." Randine stared at him.

"Yes, daughter, I understand. I will go in your place for Ola." Haagen said.

"You will bury anyone, but not accept those who need you the most. Why don't you chase down with your Ethics League, the men who get women pregnant? Teach those girls about how men use ploys like broken tokens!" Randine was almost shouting at the minister.

"How dare you show your face here." She said.

"Randine, Please." Haagen said.

The minister scowled, tipped his hat, bowed slightly and turned off the porch to visit the next house. Haagen wanted to believe that a Christian burial would do some good, but not Randine. She had to take care of Henrik after all.

As Randine was closing the door, Ursula came up the walk and greeted the two men as they were leaving, "Hello, Hr. Larstrom, Haagen. Could you tell me what happened to the corpses of the Scottish ship that went down, were some recovered? Are they being buried at sea, Reverend Larstrom?"

"Yes, most were recovered. They were returned to Scotland before the thaw." Rev. Larstrom said somberly. "The Scots wanted to bury their own, of course."

Randine brought her hand to her mouth as she gasped.

Chapter Nine
The Sisterhood

Tuesday, 24 April 1821

Dear Diary, Today I told Lena, I must have my own life so Ola does not worry about me or Henrik, so that I will not have to depend on him quite so much. I think this is sensible, but she got angry with me... Can you imagine? ...

Ursula, Randine and Lena were sitting around the fire at Ursula's, having tea in the late afternoon and trying the jam Lena had made the summer before. Lena was clearly exasperated with Randine.

"But that is what men do, they take care of their families. You must let Ola take care of you, Randine." Lena looked at Ursula with feelings of frustration.

"Lena, that is not how it will be with Ola and me, not until we are married—if we are married, and with his transfers being canceled—who knows about his promotion, when or if that will ever come through? No. I have to provide for myself. At least I might begin to learn a trade like Midwifery." She smiled widely at Ursula as she spoke. "My parents always have long ropes tied to the money they give me. It is the only way to be free of them, too."

Lena looked at Randine long and hard. "If any young woman could live by their wits, Randine, you would be the one to do it for all of us. Perhaps you are right, I just do not want to see you make life harder for yourself when there is no need. But, I understand what you say. I do understand what you ...yes, I see." Lena wrapped her arms firmly under her breasts, and grabbed one elbow.

The next day, Randine talked to Ursula as they ate breakfast.

"It seems Ursula, you are more busy than ever. Do you need more help with the births? I would so love to learn and help."

"Yes, I could. Are you sure, Randine?"

"Oh, yes, I am so eager to help."

"Alright then, for the first few months, you just watch me, stay quiet and do what I ask of you with the mothers," Ursula said very plainly. "I will only pay you for the work you are already doing, scrubbing the sheets and equipment."

Randine jumped up out of her chair and clapped her hands. Ursula held up her hands to calm Randine down.

"Then, if you show signs of this work being yours, too, I will pay you for it. Not enough for a place of your own, but enough to save. This work is not for everyone, Randine. It is very slow . . . you wait and wait for the Mother and the child in their dance with one another. Then it is very quick, and you have to be ready for the changes.

"Oh, I so want to learn."

"The pace is not up to you it is up to the baby and sometimes also the mother. The midwife is a witness of the dance between the two, mother and child. But most times, it is up to the Gods."

"Yes, how the mother and child must be in harmony."

"Sometimes they are, and well other times..., the labor is the dance they will do later together as the child grows.

"It will be good for you to earn your own money. I agree with you on this. You will feel more independent, more your own person. Who knows, if you ever move to Laerdal, perhaps you will be a midwife there. If you don't, God knows I need the help today."

Ursula knew that Randine spoke the truth, and offered her no hope of protection with men as Lena did. Ursula could be so blunt it was shocking sometimes to Randine, but it is what she liked about her, too. There was nothing but frank honesty and deep love for everyone she served. That was Ursula; clear, straight and loving.

"I have never met anyone so honest as you, Ursula. I thank you for it." Then Randine said, "I will do my best, on that, you have my word."

Ursula laughed, "Honesty and straightforward talk go with birth. Randine, birth and death do not leave room for deceptions nor laziness. What is—is. That is all. No amount of wishing will help to change what is. And, then there is the light of the mother and the child. You can tell much from this, I will teach you."

Randine scrutinized Ursula, then asked, "Do you mean the colors that I see around people sometimes? When I was pregnant, I could see rainbows, and clouds in people."

"Yes, that is part of their light. There is more, Randine, there is much I wish to share with you. Lena knows about all this, too. Perhaps we shall have a small gathering, the three of us."

Henrik began to fuss, so Randine stood up to walk him and bounce him a little.

Ursula continued, "Maybe she could come for Sunday supper. Mr. Erickson is at the tavern cleaning in the afternoon and often has his meal there. We could have a dinner here in the early afternoon, say one or two o'clock and Peter could dine with us or go on to his cleaning. I will invite them both. Maybe we could talk then once Peter is gone. I am sure Lena would enjoy it."

"Barring any babies needing to be born, or women needing preparation. I have to check on a mother near Lena's home today. I will stop and invite her and Peter over when I pass the tavern." Ursula said thoughtfully. "Did you know that Inge, another pregnant young woman with a broken token, had moved into the Erickson's bed and board?"

"No, I didn't." Randine replied, fingering her token. "Is it that common, the token?"

Ursula just looked Randine and rolled her eyes.

———————————

On Sunday, Lena and Peter arrived with some ham slices and a jar of pickled herring wrapped in a basket that Lena's mother had made for her when she was just a girl. "This is for you Randine, and for you Henrik, you will love it, it will make you a strong Viking!" Peter said with a large dose of laughter. Everyone chuckled and Lena tickled Henrik as he sat perched and wide-awake in his mother's arms. Henrik slapped the air with the laughter and giggled.

"He must like herring from Randine's milk!" Ursula chuckled.

"Everyone loves herring, it is required to be Norwegian!" Lena smiled her broad grin.

"Yes, I believe they wrote that in the new constitution a few years back!" Peter stated in mock seriousness.

"Henrik could only love it, it is what we all eat so often and well!" Randine smiled.

It was the second time that Randine had felt a real smile since giving away her own child and hearing of James's death. The first was at Christmas with her family and Ola. Still, she missed James so. It was startling to her that she could feel joy one moment and then a wave of grief the next. But now she experienced her deep sorrow more as a memory than a painful fact of every moment. But the grief, the grief still rose up, always like a tidal wave when she was alone.

They sat down to an early supper that Ursula and Randine had prepared. They ate boiled cod, and potatoes prepared with boiled cabbage and onion. For dessert they ate a pie of wild blue berries. Lena had brought Ursula a sealed jar of berries as a gift last holiday season, and she had put them in the pie.

When Ursula had guests over for supper, her dining table extended into the alcove near the front door. They had just room enough for three in the window seat, and two in chairs with Henrik on Randine's lap. Otherwise the table's leaves collapsed and made more room in one corner of the kitchen.

Most people in Bergen had the bare necessities, but not a shred more than they needed. Norway was a poor country at best. Its long history included a devastating epidemic with the black death, which caused a major decline in every facet of life in the 14th century. Some say that two thirds of the population perished. After some long centuries of struggle and poverty, Norway was trying to find its place among other countries under Danish rule. The Napoleonic wars in 1807, when Denmark and Norway entered on the side of France, devastated Norwegian trade because of restrictions and outflow of goods from Norway when it least could afford it. Denmark had ruled Norway in a congenial arrangement until Norway wanted independence. Invasions by the Swedish occurred until the Norwegians fought back hard enough to cause a cease-fire in 1809. Norway finally gained independence in 1814 only to be given to the Sweds in a deal with Denmark that was struck without Norwegian approval. It would take another 100 years before Norway was truly independent. In the winter of 1816, a winter that never left, crop production was devastated. Now, just six years later, Bergen at least was enjoying a bit more food, and some more prosperity after such suffering, with better health among most of its citizens.

Ursula's house, with room for a dining table in her kitchen, was slightly bigger than most of the houses in Bergen. Many people did not have tables at all, because they were too poor. If they did not have what they needed they went without. This is why, if a man wanted to marry a girl, he carved her a bowl and a spoon for her engagement gift. He had to show he could provide for their basic needs. In the city of Bergen, people lived in family houses with several generations. Ursula lived in a house given to her by her teacher, as she had no family left. She worked so very hard that her home was her sanctuary and now for Randine, too. She always had enough because people often paid her with food as well as skillings.

The Erickson's always had enough because they were providing food for so many at the Tavern and at the B & B. Their businesses gave them access to food at times when the common people did not have enough. Peter Erickson had learned the business from his father, and had a community of fisherman and hunters to provide for their needs. The menu changed daily, with fresh fish depending on what the local fishermen were catching. Local farmers supplied the tavern with mutton and pork.

After the dinner, Peter left for the Tavern to clean and prepare for the week. Once a week he scrubbed every surface and swept and cleaned the kitchen. He also took inventory, and a way to be alone with his thoughts while he took care of the tavern and made menus.

Henrik had fallen asleep in the low hum of conversation, and when the dishes had been done, they moved to the living room by the fire and set up three chairs in a small circle. Ursula began, "Lena, I think it is time for Randine to know about the sisterhood. She wants to become a midwife, which she has discussed with you, yes?"

"Yes, she sure has." Lena nodded, as she sat holding one elbow and cradling the other arm over her belly and under her ample breasts, her usual position for sitting in conversation.

"This one is eager." Ursula smiled.

"What is the Sisterhood?" Randine asked, her head thrust forward and head cocked so as not to miss one word of what Ursula was about to say.

"The sisterhood is not something we can tell you about. It is only to be experienced, which is why Lena and I want to share it with you. But we must be careful, people will misunderstand if they see us." Ursula rose and drew the curtains in the alcove by the door, and also closed the bedroom door just to close the space in to help everyone concentrate. She lit a candle and brought it over to the three of them, and placed it on the wooden floor in between their feet as they sat by the hearth. The fire was banked and crackling nicely.

"I will tell you this, Randine, the ancient ones speak to us; sometimes they come to speak through ... No, we will wait on that part of the story, there is time. There is time."

"Through what?!" Randine could hardly contain herself. She felt as though she was on the brink of learning something she was so hungry for. She could not wait for them to tell her.

"Nothing dear, let us show you what the Sisterhood is instead." Lena unfolded her stout arms and patted Randine on the arm. "You will see."

Lena glanced at Ursula, who nodded, then took each of them by the hand to form a circle as they sat in their chairs.

"Okay, let us call in the Sisterhood." Ursula and Lena closed their eyes, and Randine did the same, following their lead.

"From our circle of light, Freya, Mother, Sister of the sea, I call you forth, ask you to join our small circle, we three women of Bergen, come, be with us. We ask you in the name of the Futark, sacred symbol of the ancestors."

Nothing happened at first, but then Randine's head started to spin a little.

"Breathe Randine, just breathe and relax," Ursula commanded.

She took a deep breath and tried to calm herself. She felt butterflies in her stomach, feeling a little unsure, then, as she started to relax, she felt as though women in beautiful animal skins and robes were standing before them in the circle. The Goddesses were all there, Freya, and Berkana, the Valkyries. Some Valkyries looked like angels Randine once saw as a child in a Catholic bible father had imported from Italy. She could see them with her closed eyes before her.

"I, I see them!" Randine started to say.

"Shhh, listen!" Ursula commanded quietly.

"Welcome sisters, I am Freya, Mother of All. I come

to welcome this new one into our circle. Do not be afraid, Randine of the Earth and Sea, you are not here by mistake. You are one of us and belong here. You came to this Earth to carry out the work of women caring for women."

Randine saw pictures, as though in a dream flashing before her, as Freya spoke, as if she had a view into the rooms of the many she would help. She saw herself with babies crowning as women gave birth and other women in distress, she saw herself in her own birth labors and saw Ola on top of her making love, and then she saw them laughing with their children in a small cabin somewhere far away. They were in a farmhouse with others. She guessed these were his family members.

"And now, I wish to show you some pictures of your destiny to steady you on your journey." Freya waved her hand, and Randine could begin to see many women and families that she was helping. She saw strange buildings close together, not like in Bergen or anywhere she had ever visited. She saw herself with many children, she could not tell if they were her own or belonged to others and somehow it did not matter. They were all her children, all children she had helped into this world.

"As you assist life, you will also know death." Freya continued.

The pictures changed once again, and she saw an older version of herself in a strange place, a house or barn, washing the bodies of the dead. There were several men and a child. The images changed again, and she saw herself saying a prayer over a mother and her dead child, and there were other pictures of herself, mourning the dead. She shook her head, as if to get rid of so much death.

As if Freya knew what Randine was thinking, she said, "Do not fear death, it is the same gate that swings as birth, it is only a doorway."

The pictures became ribbons of bright colors waving in the wind, and she could see flashes of sun, then night, then sun again. The pictures changed again, and she could see the flowers in mountains fields in the late spring, with everything blooming. It was so beautiful she began to weep softly. Then she could see angels looking over all of it. It was then that she noticed the tears streaking her face as she touched her cheek, perhaps since the visions had begun. Her blouse was stained with tears of awe.

"Randine, my dear, call on us. Teach her, Ursula, the meaning of the Futark, Runes, speak to her of the sisterhood, how we can help others in need. Teach her Ursula, Lena, Sisters of the Stars and Sea."

As soon as Freya finished saying these words, she touched Randine on the forehead, between her eyes, and then bowed slightly, and stepped back from between the three women.

"Remember, we are always with you."

Freya's finger had burned when she touched Randine's forehead, and she could feel the imprint of a star left there. Or maybe it had always been there and Freya was showing Randine where it was? Freya disappeared.

The three women sat in the circle still holding hands. Randine noticed a slight chill in the room. It had been so warm while Freya was there with her. First Ursula squeezed Randine's hand, and then Lena, and they dropped hands.

Randine covered her face and wept, she was so overwhelmed with what Freya had showed her. She felt her destiny was revealed to her, not something she ever knew existed. Now she had to find her way. She wept for all the pictures, for the grief, she cried for all those who were invisible in the spirit world who loved her so much. Overwhelmed by the love of Freya and the Gods, she suddenly knew she would never be alone wherever she went. She felt the love around her as she felt Ursula's hand on her arm and Freya standing behind her.

When she opened her eyes, Lena and Ursula were looking at her with smiles on their faces. They each leaned over and hugged her. She felt closeness to these women at that moment that she would never know with her mother, because of her mother's enormous fear of life.

"Their love is overwhelming. But it is what we live in, a sea of love," Ursula said softly.

"I, I, know, I have never... it is as though I remembered everything I came to do, and saw it all, I saw my future...my life!" She could not restrain her tears as they streaked her face.

"Yes, we saw it too Randine, your life and we saw our own life as well," Ursula said as she licked her fingers and put out the candle. Randine noticed that the candle had burned low. They must have been in communion much longer than she felt it to be. In her mind it was just a moment yet an eternity. Randine got up to add more wood to the fire.

"Randine, you must never speak of this—nor of the Sisterhood—unless Freya herself calls you to speak of any vision you may have. Freya will come, in your dreams, or in the presence of another in the group of the Sisterhood. She will give you a sign, you will know. The other sisters will find you, as you travel, wherever you go. They will know you. No words need be spoken. Do you understand?" Ursula was more stern than usual and Randine nodded in agreement.

"Am . . . Am I a witch now?" Randine asked.

Ursula and Lena burst into laughter.

"You are not a witch! But know that, as has happened in the past, a foolish tongue can bring trouble. Some of our sisters were burned at the stake for being in the Sisterhood. They were too open about their gifts and visions."

Ursula had gone from laughter to seriousness. Randine understood. She was raised on the stories of the witches, trolls, and healers, and some people thought they were all of the devil. Though somehow, she knew this was not true.

"Those pictures I saw, they were so real. How could we . . . what just happened? Please tell me." Randine was drying her eyes on her apron, which she still wore from preparing the food.

"You have been initiated into the Sisterhood, Randine. You are part of a group of women that stretch back to
the beginning of time. It is an ancient chain, women helping
women—healers, teachers, mothers, sisters, and friends.
But not everyone can know of us—your mother, for example, as she is too much believing in the Christian way,
which locks her in her fear. Not every Christian believes as
she does, but it is not worth the risk to tell anyone, unless
they approach you or unless Freya herself comes to you.
And I tell you this, as sure as Christ had visions of his heav-
enly father, the Christian way and Freya are not separate.
Mary Magdalena was one of us, and Mary, too, but this truth
is lost in the bible of today, and no one can know about
this until it is time. The time will come when enough souls
release enough fear to feel the truth of the Sisterhood. Until
they lose their fear of life, of death. You will know them
Randine, as I know you, as clear as a bell sounding, you will
know others in the sisterhood..." Ursula said assuring her.

Ursula's words burned into Randine's heart. She
would remember this always. They will know her like a bell
sounding, as she will know them.

"Let's make a pot of tea, what do you say?" Ursula
had already gotten the water from the pitcher and poured it
into the kettle.

Lena stood up slowly, as her hips got stiff while sitting in any chair for too long.

"Thank you Ursula. Yes, tea would be good," Lena
said slowly.

Randine could not speak. The experience was still
moving through her, and she could not gather her thoughts.

"Listen my dear, I want you to understand something." Ursula drew her chair closer and put a hand on her
shoulder before putting the kettle on. Lena moved towards
the kitchen instead.

"Whatever you saw was real. The images, they are of
your life, but do not hold on to them, do not try to under-

stand these things as they may shift and change as you shift and change. Freya was showing your destiny to you, yes, and she wanted you to know that your life, however long, is already written. You made your agreements already before you came here. Still you have choices within these agreements. Live your choices from the heart, your map is there." Ursula pointed to Randine's chest. "This way you have nothing to fear, just follow your heart and you will live out your destiny as sure as you see these pictures today. Do you understand?"

"But, but wait, don't we have free will? I have so many questions." Randine felt she would burst.

Lena returned from the latrine in the back yard and brought in more water from the pump outside in the yard. Then she threw some wood into the firebox of the cookstove to get the heat started again. She placed the water in the kettle on the iron plate.

"Thank you dear," Ursula said to Lena, then turned back to Randine.

"Yes, you have free will. AND, some of your choices were laid out before you came as you are here to do service for others. On this you have already agreed. But, how that service is done and how often, that is what you must decide in your heart. What you saw was for you to know as an invisible map laid out for you in your heart. You can share it if you want with us." Lena said.

Lena's invitation helped Randine. The kettle whistled and she poured some hot water into the Ursula's lovely flowered teapot and swirled it to warm the pot. She dumped it out into a bowl and then put some chamomile leaves in the teapot and poured in more water to steep them. Then they sat there together and Randine began to tell them what she saw.

"This is what I know. Ola and I are destined to be together. We will have many children. Some will live and some will not. Oh heaven forbid! We will not always live here, but in a bigger city, and also in the wilderness near the fjords.

There are many people I will care for, and some I will bury. But, but, I do not love Ola, and he is only doing his duty by Henrik and me! Though I know he loves his son. I am so confused!"

"Yes, tell us no more, the rest you should keep in your own heart," Lena said, drawing Randine's vision closed with a wave of her hand.

"But there is something else. I saw, saw, my own spirit, too, looking over everyone from above. How can that be? Could this be at the same time as the other pictures? I—I don't understand."

"We cannot always know what these visions mean. Don't try to figure them out. Heavens, no, just feel what is true for you in your heart. Let the rest go. One way to see this is that you will oversee hundreds of lives, Randine. Another, that you will watch over others after you die. It could have been a view from your soul, which is very large. It is possible to travel out of the body and view oneself from that vantage point. I feel we do this in our dreams. We do not know what window or doorway will take us into the spirit world. There are many windows, and many doors, and not always the ones we see in the pictures, Randine," Ursula said plainly. "We always have free will to change or disregard what we know in our hearts. But be open. While there are agreements that we make before our birth, these things do not always happen in life. Everything can change, including your feelings."

"Yes, Randine, we are like cats with many lives. You, too, my dear, have many lives." Lena chuckled as she looked at Ursula and winked.

"I remember when I was first initiated," Lena began, "My mother had died in childbirth with my brother many years before. My first blood came, and I knew nothing about what it was. A neighbor woman, bless her soul, she took me aside and initiated me as we did today. Freya came and she told me many things, and let me know that I am at one with the Sisters. I saw my house, Peter, the tavern, and many young women coming here, some would be initiated and some not. But I carry Freya's mark, here."

Lena pointed to her forehead and Randine saw her wrinkled brow, then a flame appeared as clear as if she had a fire in her forehead.

"Yes, and I have it too." Ursula leaned in and pointed to her forehead. Randine again saw nothing, then she saw the flame, plain as day. "It is how you know us, Randine, now you have one too. How we knew you."

She felt her forehead, and the skin was smooth. She knew it was there, but could not touch it with her hand nor mind. Yet the star burned brightly as a flame when she closed her eyes and felt her love rise in her heart.

"It is inside, this is how you will know," Lena said softly. "Just look with your heart, not your head."

"Everyone has them, dear, they just get shrouded by fear and anger. Every woman on this Earth could be in the Sisterhood, if they would just release the fear and shame that the religions teach."

Henrik started to wake up from his nap and Randine could feel her breasts getting ready to feed him. She unbuttoned her blouse, picked up her son and settled in again to feed him.

"Is there a Brotherhood, too?" Randine asked, as she sat down with Henrik and he found her nipple.

"Yes, but too few men know of it," Ursula said with a sigh. "It is there, waiting for them. The Gods hold the healthy male for all men. Jesus was, is one, so was Thor, and all the male Gods. Yes, there are men who know, but they are fewer and further between than the women. Women are closer to the Earth, and closer to Freya because of their wombs bleeding every month and giving birth. "

Randine looked at Henrik nursing. *He looks so peaceful, so perfect.*

"How will he know if he is one of us, of the Brotherhood, I mean?" Randine asked.

Ursula went on. "The Sons of Norway are the sons of this land. They originally were part of the Brotherhood.

There are those called Masons, who care for the mysteries. Scots have their temples, the Templars. Some have become focused onto war. But most are lovers of the Earth, and of the mysteries that live all around us. It has to do with their love of country, of people, their lack of fear of life. They must see life as a great adventure, not as something to be woefully feared. Launch Henrik into life, and life will tell him whether fear rules him or love. In the meantime, Randine, know one more thing. You are no different than the ones with fear, or the other sisters or brothers who would burn you. All are equal. All are part of Freya, Thor, and the Familyhood of life. Some know love as their teacher, and some are afraid of love. That is the only difference between us. I am glad you could receive Freya's love. Her message is the message of love. That is the real importance within you. You are that love, Randine. Don't let any one tell you different." Ursula drank the last of the tea in her cup and stood up to take her cup to the kitchen.

"It is time for me to go. I have to check on that old man down the road," Lena said. "Don't get up, dear, feed your baby. Ursula, let us get together soon." Lena bent over and kissed Randine on top of the head. "There is more Randine, much more."

Then she kissed Ursula, too, and the two women walked to the door together, talking low so Randine could not hear.

"Watch your dreams, Lena, there is more, much more," Ursula said as she walked Lena out onto the front porch the sun lowering in the sky.

"Yes, I know this is true. I will light a candle for Freya tonight." Lena smiled.

Henrik was sleeping now at Randine's breast, his little jaw still working then stopping, working then stopping. Randine thought, 'If I am love, so is he.' She looked at Ursula standing in the door, greeting a neighbor as she waved goodbye to Lena. 'So is she. So are we all.'

Just then, Henrik woke up and reached for her face.

His hand landing on her neck, his touch brought her around again to him. She grabbed his little hand with her free hand and kissed his tiny fingers. He smiled his big love smile.

Randine thought of Ursula's words, "We are all the same." She thought also of her hatred for the church for rejecting her after her pregnancy. But as she thought of them in their fearful beliefs she felt compassion for them, and her anger and hatred faded. She nursed Henrik in spite of his loving grin. Then she thought of her mother, and of the hard feelings she had towards both her parents. Again, those feelings seemed to melt when she recalled Ursula's words, 'They are just like you only with fear.' But where were they when she needed them? Again, she felt her heart harden, then soften, as she nursed Henrik. The anger faded in the face of love, Henrik's love for his mother, and Randine's love for him.

Chapter Ten
Randine's First
Midwifery Day

Monday, 30th April 1821
Dear Diary, Today I got to help Ursula with my first birth!
What a miracle it is, how difficult the ordinary life can be...

Randine woke with a sudden excitement to get up and go to her first appointment with Ursula. After feeding Henrik and preparing a sling with lamb's wool she wore around her neck and over one shoulder, tucking him in, she set out to find Ursula. Lena was at the Tavern, cleaning and sweeping from the night before. Randine stopped there because she could not find the street where Ursula had gone to attend a birth, and Lena knew every street in Bergen.

She caught up with Ursula at Mrs. Jensatter's house. Mrs. Jensatter was a widow who opened her home for young women in a crisis. Mrs. Jensatter had begun her effort when her own daughter died in childbirth at age fourteen. She had lost her grandson, too. Widowed a few years before, she realized with her daughter's death that she had no family, that her own attitudes were to blame for pushing her daughter away when she needed help the most. Now, she was taking care of those young girls that society shamed and no one else would have.

When Randine arrived, Mrs. Jensatter was warm and welcoming. "Hello Randine, Ursula is in the first room there, on your right. How are you and your baby boy?"

"Just fine Mrs. Jensatter, Ursula is taking good care of us. Henrik sleeps so well anywhere..." Randine whispered, pointing to her shawl where Henrik was cradled.

"Good," Mrs. Jensatter whispered back. "The Lord

has taken good care of you."

Randine wondered if it was it the Lord, or Freya, or just good luck? But she dare not utter such words in this house or any other Lutheran home, as she would be called a heretic.

When she knocked at the bedroom door where Ursula was, she heard a moan and then someone saying to come in. Ursula was waiting for a girl to give birth sitting in a chair by the fire. She was not much younger than Randine. The young woman was walking around, squatting from time to time to relieve her back, and moaning.

"Well, hello Randine! How nice to see you," Ursula said warmly. "Come in, this is Helga. She is preparing as you can see, but it is going to be a little while yet."

Helga bent slightly from the waist to acknowledge Randine standing in the doorway, but had her hands around her belly to relieve the weight and kept walking. The room was spacious, with a double bed on one wall and a large draped window across from the door. A sheet covered the pine floors where the birthing stool was placed next to the fireplace. A small table and four chairs were next to the bed as Randine came into room.

"Come sit, Helga. This is Randine. Where is Henrik?"

"Here," Randine pointed to her sling.

"Good, this is good, babies always reach out to babies who are coming. Would you like some tea, Randine? Helga? Mrs. Jensatter just made some."

"Yes, yes that would be good." It was obvious to Ursula that Randine had something on her mind.

Randine was watching Helga as she paced back and forth. She took her shawl and put it over the mother-to-be.

Ursula watched Randine and then said, "Yes, Helga, keep warm while you pace, and remember to breathe. Come join us if it feels well to do so."

"Ursula you are like a cat, with one eye on Helga, and one on me. I won't stay long."

"It is not to worry, Helga is doing just fine. You can

stay," Ursula stated as she poured a cup of tea for Randine and Helga.

"Ursula, am I starting my apprenticeship with you today?"

Ursula had gotten up from her chair and helped Helga to a stand after squatting again. Young Helga had a contraction.

"Breathe Helga, breathe dear," Ursula commanded.

After the contraction, Helga resumed her slow pacing, and Randine continued.

"Ursula, what I want to say, what I want to ask—if there is anything I can do, please just tell me. I want to understand what you are doing, I want to learn about midwifery."

Ursula paused. "Hmm, I see—that is it. Helga you are doing fine, come have some tea, dear, it will calm you a bit."

Helga came and sat at the edge of the chair, as she sipped the tea and it was the first Randine had seen her face. Randine saw how young she was, even younger than she herself. Not a pretty girl, she was stout and had fear in her face. Ursula addressed Randine.

"Yes, dear, you are beginning today. I do want your help. My only concern is that it might be too soon for you, after your own birthing." Ursula looked into Randine's eyes very deeply. Randine knew she was referring to the losses of James and her son.

"You know this is my busy time. I have another woman about to deliver down the street, and two more over near the lake. I am using the women's own sheets more and more if they have them. It saves us from doing so much laundry. And you can take Henrik with you to play with the other children while you are with the mothers."

"Well, I want to help. What you did for me was so special. I want to give that to other women." Randine looked down at her hands folded in her lap to hold back tears. She had never felt so passionate about anything before. It is as though her desire to serve other women was a fire burning inside her. She was embarrassed by her own trembling voice.

"Yes," Ursula said calmly placing a hand on her shoulder, "I understand your wishes. If you would start with me tomorrow, perhaps Lena can watch Henrik, or you can bring him along. As I said, a baby helps other babies to come more quickly, I think."

Just then Helga doubled over and moaned. The contractions were strong.

"Here, Randine, take Helga's arm. Let us get her to the birthing stool, where at least she can rest and still sit a bit."

Ursula grabbed the "U" shaped birthing stool, and Randine moved with Helga slowly.

"There is no reason to rush." Ursula said.

The birthing stool was a horseshoe-shaped low stool with four sturdy legs that helped to stabilize the sitting. The center was missing so that the baby could come through. It was the shape of a new moon.

Helga looked at Randine and began to cry, "I don't think I can do this, Miss. I don't know how this baby will ever come out!" She wailed.

"Helga, I know how you feel. I just gave birth a few months ago. But you can do it. If I can, you can," Randine said, as she stroked Helga's hair. "Look, I am smaller in the hips than you." Randine stood and smiled, showing her behind.

"Randine you are a natural midwife already. This is your first lesson. Reassuring Helga is the best thing you can do for her. Tell her the truth, and encourage her. But never lie. Never tell them it is all right when it isn't. A pregnant woman is full of instinct, and she will know you lied. Then your trust is gone. Your trust is the safety the baby is born into."

"You see Helga, what Randine said is true. You are born to give birth, you have a wonderful sturdy body for giving birth, and you will be a wonderful loving mother."

"OHHH! Here comes another one!" Helga screamed.

"Randine, can you stay a few more minutes?" Ursula asked. "I think Helga might have her baby now."

"Yes, of course."

"OHHH NOOO!" Helga shouted. "I'm not ready!"

"Helga, look at me," Randine said brushing her hair back and leaning into Helga's face. "You can do this, I am here, and I won't leave you. See? Here is my sleeping boy."

Ursula was sitting on the floor in front of Helga, and had lifted her dressing gown to check on Helga's progress. Randine was standing behind Helga now, rubbing her back, and singing a low song to keep Henrik sleeping.

"You can do it, Helga, you can do it. Go deeper, and now let this baby come into the world," Ursula said calmly.

Randine shifted Henrik in his little sling to her back so she could hold Helga from the back and she could squeeze her hands. Randine gave Helga her chest to rest against as she knelt behind her.

"AHHHHHH!" Helga shouted. She grabbed Randine's hands, and held them tightly. Helga's body-sweat and breath filled Randine's nostrils.

"Look, the head is coming out." Ursula took one of Helga's hands from Randine's so she could feel her child's head crowning.

"Helga, on the next contraction, push but wait, wait for the big wave."

Helga was panting hard, and suddenly the wave came," EEHHHH!"

"Look your baby's head is out.

"Okay, on the next one, here your baby comes."

Ursula caught the child as Helga pushed.

Helga gripped Randine's hands, and screamed on the last contraction. Out slid her little girl. With her skilled hands, Ursula grabbed the towel she always carried over her shoulder during births and wiped clean the mouth and head and wrapped the baby with a soft blanket in a few swift movements and handed her to Helga.

When Helga saw her daughter's face, she let go of

Randine's hands and reached to hold her baby. Randine knelt behind her and leaned her body against Helga to support her back while leaning over her shoulder to see the new baby. Helga cleaned her mouth with the corner of the cloth as Ursula rubbed the back of the child with her hand. The color of the baby changed in Helga's arms from blue to bright red, as her daughter took her first breath, and began to wrinkle her face into a scream. Ursula and Randine took the rest of the gown off as it had a large slit down the front. As Helga sat on the stool they were able to lift it over her head. Randine wrapped the dressing gown around Helga's shoulders to keep her and the baby warm.

"You see? Here she is! You did it!" Randine said excitedly.

"My daughter, my little Ursula Randine!" Helga said with tears in her eyes.

"This one wanted to come right now!" Ursula stated. "She came much faster than I thought she would."

"Helga was smiling ear to ear. Ursula, thank you, thank you so much. Randine, thanks to you too! I could not have done this without both of you."

"We are not done yet. One more push when you feel the next wave, and let that after-birth out." Ursula said.

Helga's face changed, as she felt the wave of contraction. Then she focused on the tidal wave of energy moving through her, took a breath and pushed. Out slid the after-birth, with some blood and fluid. Ursula had placed a cloth underneath her to catch the placenta and the blood.

"Time to make your birthing stew," Ursula stated cutting the cord. "Randine, take this to Mrs. Jensatter, and ask her to make a birthing stew for Helga, along with some butter porridge."

Randine carried the bloody placenta in the washbasin out of the room, while Ursula cleaned Helga, and then helped her to the bed.

"There now, you need to rest," Randine heard Ursula say as she left the room.

Randine noticed the sun was low in the sky as she called out to Mrs. Jensatter, and realized that she had been with Ursula and Helga longer than she had anticipated.

She found Mrs. Jensatter in the kitchen preparing a meal for the girls, with several other pregnant girls helping. Mrs. Jensatter was delighted by the news of the birth.

Then she introduced Randine to the other girls, and all of them seemed shy and embarrassed. Randine set two of the girls to work slicing the placenta for Helga's stew.

"How is your son, Randine," Mrs. Jensatter asked to calm the girls embarrassment, Randine hesitated then looked at Mrs. Jensatter.

"Oh he is just fine, he is asleep on my back." Randine shifted Henrik carefully and gently around so they could see him sleeping. The girls smiled and nodded."It is good to meet you, and nice to meet you all. Good luck with your babies! My son is the light of my life. See?"

Randine left the kitchen, and returned to Helga's room where she in bed with her baby. Ursula smiled as Randine came back into the room to say goodbye.

"Thank you for your help Randine, tomorrow we shall meet two houses down. Mrs. Johndatter Johns. She is about to give birth, too. I will be checking her tomorrow, mid-morning.

Randine smiled at Ursula. "I have so many questions, can we talk some tomorrow too?"

"Yes, between calls, we can walk fast and talk."

"Randine!" Helga said. "Thank you, thank you so for your help!"

"Yes, you have a fine daughter, little Ursula Randine!" Randine bent to kiss Helga on the head, and stroked the child lightly on the cheek.

Randine smelled the lavender in the air that Ursula had burned just as she had at her own birth of James. Randine felt a rush of sadness come over her as the smell reminded her of her own darling son who she gave away, and wondered how he was and if he was healthy.

"I will see you tomorrow Ursula, or tonight," Randine said, leaving the room. Her eyes burned and she began to cry. Henrik began to stir and Randine checked him for a dirty diaper. He was waking up, and not at all wanting to be in the sling any more.

"Just a little longer, son." Randine wiped her tears and shifted the sling around to the front, and gave him her breast to suckle. Then she covered him, and walked as fast she as she dare down the stairs and across the cobblestone street in front of the house. Lena would be expecting her for dinner as their guest tonight. Randine thought of all the things she wanted to ask Ursula. How do you know when the baby is coming? What tells you to get her to the birthing stool? How far apart are the contractions when they are ready? What is the reason for the birthing stool, as she did not use it with her birth? What was the reason she told Helga she had a long time yet, when she gave birth so suddenly? How do these girls find Mrs. Jensatter? How many does she have there? Who is it that pays their way? How does Ursula get paid? Does she deliver all the babies at Mrs. Jensatter's house?

The questions trailed off, and a thousand more came up, as Randine reached the door to Lena's house. As she entered the house and she set Henrik down to play on the floor with a wooden spoon and bowl, as Lena bent over the stew pot on the stove. Without turning around, she said,

"Randine how was your day, dear?"

"Lena you won't believe it! I have a job with Ursula. I started today! Lena, I am going to be a midwife, isn't that wonderful!"

Chapter Eleven
The Letting Go Ritual

Thursday, 29 November 1821
Randine's Diary
It has been one year since James died. Today is the day before
Henrik was born and a few days past the birth of little James.
It feels as though I walk two feet under the ground through
mud. My feelings are so mixed up. I cried all morning. I am
glad Ola is not due back for a while.

Ursula took Randine down to the breakwater near
the end of the harbor. They walked a long way along the
shore with Henrik on Randine's back. Ursula had asked her
to bring something that reminded Randine of James. Something special he might have given her that she was holding
on to. Randine always wore the broken token he had given
her, so she brought that along with the spoon he had carved
for her. This was their betrothal spoon. He was to make a
bowl, too, had he lived. She could not think of why Ursula
would want her to bring these things from James.

When they arrived at the farthest end of the harbor past the jetty, the wind was cold, but it was clear for
a change and bright. Bergen was overcast so much of the
time. These few hours of sunlight were welcome and warm-
ing them nicely. Henrik was sleeping when they got to the
rocks. They took him out of the carrier on Randine's back.
While she laid him down beside the basket of food they had
brought she sheltered him from the cold with a shawl. Then
with another small blanket, Randine made a little tent with
the second shawl, to keep him out of the wind.

Ursula took Randine's hands, called in the four directions announcing to the world,

"Today we were here to mourn and release Randine's lover James MacGregor."

The wind stopped while Ursula spoke and the water seemed to calm. She took a golden straw wreath from her satchel. Randine wondered when she had any time at all to make this? The wreath had black ribbon spiraling around it with tiny figures on each side—a man on one side and a baby in a cradle on the other. Then she began to sing a lament that people sang when there was a loss. It was an ancient song that had no words really, more of a deep moaning sound that started high and went low into her heart. Randine tried to join her, but she could not sing. Randine could not let go of James more than she had. She was at the bottom of her grief drowning.

When she finished, and asked Randine to tie the spoon and the necklace from James to the wreath. It broke her heart open again, but James was gone and he wasn't coming back and neither her baby. The necklace was for James, the spoon for their child.

Ursula sang another song of release and motioned to Randine to go to the ocean. Randine slowly and carefully crawled out over the rocks that made the breakwater. She stood above the water on a rock that stretched out over the sea. When Ursula hit a high note and Randine was ready, she tossed the wreath out as far as possible. The wind picked up at that very moment and carried it out further than Randine could ever have thrown it. She sank down on the rock and wept like she had never wept before. She felt the wind come up again and watched it push the wreath out in the swift choppy water beyond retrieving. Randine said goodbye to her dear James, and it was over. Then deep from the soles of her feet she felt a wail come up, a scream, it was as though the earth itself was screaming. The scream ripped through her as if she was in labor.

Then she realized there had been no funeral for James except for one memorial for all the men who were lost in his ship. Because of Henrik she could not attend and couldn't have brought herself to go anyway. She could not go to any service in the Lutheran church as she swore she would not step one foot in there again. James and his crew were mourned in Scotland where he and the crew and the ship in which they sailed were from. When Randine finally brought herself to crawl off the rocks, Ursula waved her hand in each direction to open the circle of the four directions. Randine could hear Henrik fussing and went to him.

"My dear Henrik, what would I do without you?"

Randine picked up her son, and the three of them sat on the shawls. They ate a bite of cheese and bread and some dried fish in silence.

On the long walk home Randine felt more easy and free in her step and less burdened. She was not slogging through mud anymore, and James' memory seemed just that, a memory. She was still sad at his loss, and her son's adoption, but there was no turning back the clock. Henrik was fussing and wanted to play with her hair so they played pony with her hair on the way home. She felt a hundred pounds lighter. When they got home, she and Ursula made a cake to celebrate Henrik's birthday the next day.

Chapter Twelve
The Initiation Ceremony

Thursday, 1 May 1823
Dear Diary, Ola said he would be coming back this summer
in his last letter, I hope his ship sails safely and he catches a
good breeze. Today was the most amazing day of my life. I
will never forget it as long as I live!

Ola had been gone most of the previous year and much of this one. His orders had changed again, and again, and Randine and Henrik had only seen him a few times on leave between assignments. Ola had promised in his letters he would be coming this summer through Bergen, and perhaps he could finally speak of his plans to her and bring her to Laerdal.

Randine would be eighteen in the late fall, though she looked as though she could pass for twenty. Ursula had trained Randine well, so that now she could easily take a call for Ursula if she was called to two places at once. They had done many births together, and seen all sorts of issues arise. Randine was much more steady with the women and the babies. She wore a clear air of confidence.

On May Day, the town bloomed with the first signs of spring. Some celebrated in the local districts by decorating the houses with fresh flowers, and some used dried flowers, if the winter was too harsh, to decorate their cattle, and houses, sleighs and wagons.

Spring-cleaning in the city had much to do with these festivities, and the ancient broom was used to sweep the old out the house and guard the house from unwanted spirits. Most rested a broom for the day outside the front door to keep away evil spirits. Old traditions die hard, and Bergen like in most places was set in its old pagan ways despite the church.

    Ursula and Randine were cleaning out her home. Everything had to be aired outside, or tossed out the windows to clean off any bugs or fleas. Hay mattresses were left outside for the whole day, the hay stuffing was burned to kill any lice or other creatures. They restuffed with new hay that had been frozen in the winter barns.

    Randine was busy finishing the stuffing of her new mattress, when Ursula called her inside the house for a moment. She took the last stitch to the end of it, to seal it up, and threw it over the laundry line that was stretched across the back of the house.

    Henrik was chewing on a cherry twig that he had found under the tree in the back of the house. There was nowhere for him to go, with the fence all around the yard, and nothing for him to get into, so she left him alone for a moment as she stood on the back step, keeping one eye on him as she answered Ursula's call.

    "What is it Ursula? Is there a call for us to go to someone?"

    "No Randine, bring Henrik, we want you to come with us."

    She picked up her son and took the stick out of his mouth. Black bark speckled his red lips, and he drooled with a big smile. He was teething, and anything he could find to help cut his teeth was a relief.

    When she entered Ursula's house, her mother was there with Lena and Ursula. Lena and Ursula had not seen each other for sometime, even though there was a new woman in Lena's boarding house about to give birth in the next few days. But the two of them had not forgotten their promise to Randine to offer her the ceremony they had wanted to give her. This was the next ceremony they had to do for Randine before she left with Ola, if that would be happening this summer. At least that is what they saw in the vision given to them by Freya.

    It became clear to Ursula from her conversations

with Randine that she was ready. She would soon be eighteen and it would be good for her to have her initiation before she left for Laerdal. Then she could pass it on to others if she saw fit. This was the second ceremony Ursula wanted to give her dear apprentice.

"Randine, your mother has agreed to take Henrik for the afternoon. Lena and I want to take you to collect herbs."

Randine stood still for a moment and looked at her two elder mentors. They were both grinning, and had a lunch basket already prepared as it sat on the kitchen table. Her mother was eager to have Henrik for a whole day, as she had missed mothering so and loved being a grandmother.

"What about milk for Henrik?" Randine asked, confused. Did we get any from the farmer today?" she asked Ursula. She hadn't been apart from him more than a few hours in the two and a half years, especially for feedings and she was nervous to leave him alone.

"Your mother will provide him some goat milk later, he can eat cheese and grains now, he will be all right. We won't be gone that long." Ursula couldn't help but smile.

"Something is going on between you two," Randine said, shaking her finger at them.

"Alright, if you insist." Randine sat Henrik down in her mother's lap. The three older women chatted about the weather, and the spring, as May is such a wonderful time to do house cleaning. But Randine knew something else was going on.

They left the house after Henrik was sleeping soundly. He was at such a clingy stage, yet she knew her mother would care for him well. She would stay at Ursula's as his few toys were at Ursula's scattered around the living room.

The Test

Lena and Ursula began to walk out of town, and Randine followed, but said little. Lena was chattering away about something to Ursula that Randine could not hear from behind them anyway, so Randine decided to be with herself.

The three of them took a trail Randine had not known about. They were not on a mail route road, nor were they heading to any place Randine had ever been before. At a fork in the road, Ursula stopped with Lena as they discussed where to go. At least it wasn't raining, Randine thought.

"I think we go right, or is it left? Lena, I cannot remember."

"We go to the right, always the right."

"I don't know, I think perhaps left."

"Left will take you down below away from where we planned the picnic. No, we want to go right."

"Where are we going? What are you two up to?" Randine inquired.

"It's a surprise!" The two women answered in unison.

Randine was startled by their answer. They had planned something for sure.

"But maybe we want to take the trail going down first, then climb up towards the top near the birch grove."

"That would be backwards! We have to go right first, then below," Lena argued.

She was clearly getting more upset with Ursula. Lena's hands were on her hips, and she was leaning forward stubbornly pushing towards her friend.

"No, this is not the way, I am sure of it. We MUST go left first, then we can end at the birches."

"End what?" Randine asked again. This time she wanted to know what was going on.

The two ignored her and continued arguing.

"If you want to go below first then you go, and take your stupid basket with you. We are going to the right and that is final," Lena said, with her nose two inches from Ursula's face.

"Fine, if that is the way you want it!" Ursula was shouting now.

"Fine! Come on Randine!" Lena shouted back.

Randine stood at the crossroads of the juncture of two trails and stared at Ursula's back as she tromped off down the trail and disappeared into the forest.

"Wait, Ursula, where are you going?" Randine did not understand what they were doing. She and Lena seemed to be ending their friendship over such a simple decision. Right or left. She turned to Lena, but she was already down the trail and almost disappeared. Randine noticed the basket for lunch left behind.

"Lena, wait, the basket!" Randine shouted. Without thinking, she picked up the basket and ran after Lena, but then she felt she was supposed to go with Ursula, she ran back to the trail crossing again. Ursula was completely out of sight. She ran back to the juncture, this time going down the left fork, then she stopped and walked backwards towards the crossroads and stood alone for a moment.

"Now what!" Randine began to cry, and sat down in middle of the earthen trail setting down the basket beside her. She began to feel abandoned. There she was in a place she did not know, and she had no idea what to do. Right or left, right, left? She was so startled by the argument, by their strange behavior, and had been so caught up in it she could not make up her mind at all.

She sat in the trail and whipped her tears for a moment. Suddenly she thought to look in the basket. There was bread and cheese and a few boiled eggs, and some dried fish and dried cherries from Ursula's tree. But that was only on the top layer, on the bottom layer, under another cloth, there was a bag tied with a string, and some herbs under the bag in small bundles. There were two sticks, and a piece of chalk.

"What are these here for?" she found herself saying out loud. Randine took the bag out of the basket and untied it. Tipping the contents of the bag out on her hand, she saw several runes. These weren't Ursula's or Lena's runes. She brushed aside the thought that she did not recognize them, and instead looked at which ones had fallen out. They were marked with the familiar signs. The first was a line marked down the center. "Standstill, well that is accurate." She was at a standstill. The second was the rune for gateway, the third for initiation.

Then she realized that she was not using these runes properly, for they held much power. She recognized the herbs as dried lavender, chamomile, and sage. Suddenly she realized she was having her womanhood ceremony. The birth was an initiation, so were the losses, but this was the secret initiation into the Sisterhood that they had hinted about when she first met Freya. She was in the ceremony already! That was why Lena and Ursula had pretended to have their fight, why she was left here, holding this bag and the basket alone.

Taking a deep breath, Randine stood up and found the East with the dull glow of it's sun through the clouds, then knelt and cleared a space for herself at the crossroads. She centered herself, then drew a chalk circle around herself. Pictures returned from Freya's vision gifts. She stood in the middle of the chalk circle. Then she felt a cord of light moving from the top of her head into her heart and from her heart into the Earth. She was connected with the Sky and Earth, as Ursula had instructed her. Breathing into her heart and feeling centered there, she felt a peace once again.

Placing the two sticks on the ground inside the circle in which she stood she began drawing another circle around the sticks. Her small circle made a wheel of life, the circle with the equidistant cross in it, the four seasons, the four directions, the four races of humanity. Randine began her ceremony with a prayer.

She noticed that these sticks had been stripped of

their bark, and a small notch had been carved halfway their length to have them fit tightly together. She laid the runes that had fallen out of the bag in the East, in the place of new beginnings. She sat in the South, the place of family, birth and death. It was her direction after all. Taking a small bit of sage and lavender between her hands, she rubbed them together and brushed her energy field down along the sides of her body to clear her field of any unwanted energy. Then she took another deep breath, pulled out a hair and offered it to a plant. After waiting for a 'yes' from the plant, she thanked it. She plucked three new leaves from a plant on the trail, held them in her hand, and prayed again.

"Goddess of Earth, Fire, Water and Goddess of Air, help me find my way." She tossed the leaves in the air, and they landed in or on the line of the North, clearly marking the trail that Lena had trodden.

"Thank you!" Randine said out loud. "I'll take the path to the right."

She bowed her head to the center of the cross, touching her forehead on the crossed pieces. Carefully placing the runes back in the sack, she picked up the sticks and placed them in the bag, rubbing the chalk into the earth with her foot.

Placing the items in the picnic basket, she trotted off down the trail that Lena had taken. Her ears and eyes were wide open with excitement. Beyond the bushes and trees where Lena dissapeared, Ursula stayed hidden until Randine was out of sight.

"Good, she has passed the first test," Ursula thought.

Randine stopped at the edge the woods. "HMMM, gracious lord of the woods, may I enter?" Randine prayed. She felt an unseen presence by her right shoulder, and a gentle spirit's hand on her back, encouraging her to enter the woods. Stepping into the woods on the trail with her right foot, she walked forward with slow and deliberate steps.

Soon down the trail she heard rushing water. She could smell the freshness of the river. The closer she got to river the more she heard the thundering of a waterfall, but could not see it. She knew from Ursula's stories, that this was the place where they initiated all the women. It was the place Ursula had been brought to for her initiation when she first moved to Bergen.

Randine stopped again. "Goddess of the river, may I come to you?" She waited. Then with a rush of wind and a soft touch on her cheek of a drop of dew from a leaf above she felt the answer. She bowed low from her waist and drew closer to the stream. Soon she could see a footbridge that guided her to the other side.

She was not going to fool around with this initiation, so she stopped at the log bridge and looked around. There on the branch overhead was a feather tied on with a string. It was from a little bird that lived near this river. Lena or Ursula had left it for her as a sign that she was on the right track. Looking around before she stepped on the bridge to see if anyone there, she could hear only the thundering of the falls, but she was certain she was going in the right direction. Crossing the log bridge carefully, she looked at the rushing water below. She could see that not far from where she crossed, the falls disappeared over a ledge.

On the other side of the trail she found a twig that had been bent, pointing down another trail that seemed to go to the bottom of the falls. She walked slowly, looking for more signs, noting animal tracks and any broken branches. She noticed bird tracks in the mud and a place where it pecked for food. A dog, or possibly wolf tracks were at edge of the trail. Then she noticed the claw marks. She pushed the thought away. Must be a dog. Through raining falls she heard little else but the falls thundering. Randine climbed down steep rocks and boulders, and slid part way down to the trail at the bottom following the forty-foot waterfall.

It was magnificent, and it was in the woods, completely hidden from trails or roads. At the bottom, she found another sign left by her mentors. Small rocks had been stacked and pointed to the falls. This completely stumped her. She sat on a boulder and studied the falls. At first she noticed how the water was hitting huge slabs of rock. The water tumbled off of everything. Then, to the left of the falls, she noticed that the sheets of water did not touch the wall of the cliff behind them. There was an empty space behind the curtain of water. Finally she ventured closer, avoiding being soaked altogether, and she saw that there was a path just behind the falls. She took the basket in her left hand to keep it as dry as possible and steadied herself on a fir tree that stood at the base of the falls. There was no place to grab hold, so with her right hand, she balanced herself, until her foot landed on a stone just around the sheeting water. There, she could see a cave behind the waterfall. As she stepped around the falls, the thundering was tremendous, and she could hear nothing else but the water. Inside the cave there was much less noise.

The Ceremony

The water was cold as ice, but one more step and she was inside. She heard a crackling sound of twigs burning, and smelled smoke. Then in the darkness she saw Lena and Ursula. They were sitting near a small fire they had somehow constructed, completely dry and grinning.

"Welcome! Surprise! You made it!" Ursula laughed.

"And you found your rune stones!" Lena chuckled.

Randine had never seen her two elder friends so playful. They were like children chiding her.

"Yes, I-I thought you left me... but I see we have begun my ceremony?" Randine grinned.

"Ya, Ya, come sit." Lena said.

There by the fire was a stone for her to sit on. As her eyes adjusted to the cave's light, she could see rune marks and drawings on the back walls; the trickle of water could be heard near the back of the cave forming a small creek that ran down the center of the cave. The cave was large enough for the three of them to sit in a small circle next to rocky outcropping near the cave's creek bed. Wisps of smoke seemed to be drawn out of the cave by the draft that moved from the back of the cave to the falls in the front. Sheets of water glowed with the afternoon light. The sun was still high in the sky.

"What is this place? How did you find it? What are we going to do now?" Randine asked as she sat down.

"Too many questions. Come, sit," Lena beckoned.

Randine eased herself onto the rock. She noticed the fire must have dried their clothes well, as neither of them had a trace of wet, except at the hem of the skirts. Randine was soaked on her feet, knees and the hem of her dress and waited patiently for them to speak. Then she noticed they both had their eyes closed. She closed hers too, and went into her heart for a moment to ease herself after the anxiety of losing her friends for a while. She could perceive her heart garden there. Randine stood with a younger version of herself, a child of five, as Ursula had taught her. In this place she could go and be alone with herself as a child where she could calm herself and bring in peace. It was the child that was upset, and now calm. Instantly she felt better, and knew they were here to begin a most important moment for her. Ursula began to speak. Her voice seemed low and serious now.

"Go inside your heart in your garden, Randine, good you are already there. Breathe into your heart, and see that we are meeting you there."

She took a deep breath and moved away from her worried thoughts and felt the ease in her heart's garden. Another breath took her deeper. She was feeling herself moving down into her body. A place was there, still at first, then she saw a gate and row of trees lining the garden inside her heart. At the gate, Lena and Ursula were standing waiting for her.

"Good, now invite your wildness in."

Randine did not know what they meant. Wildness. Hmmm, she took another deep breath and soon a wolf came to the gate and stood next to them. She opened the gate for the wolf and she was not afraid. This wolf seemed friendly, not the wolves of childhood stories that frightened her so much when she was little.

"Good, now invite in your wise mother."

Randine set her intention for this wise mother, who-ever she was, to come to her. She waited. Then slowly, she saw her standing behind Ursula and Lena. She opened the gate at the front, and the woman stepped through. She was an older version of Randine. But she noticed that she was strong and gentle.

"That is good!" Lena sighed. "She is a strong one. Now call in Mother Frigg, she wants to meet you in person." Her voice had a touch of humor in it.

Randine took another breath. She tried to calm her mind—Frigg, the mother Goddess, in her heart?"

She let go of her thoughts and stood by her wise mother and her wolf inside the fence that separated her from Ursula and Lena. She felt a breeze on her face, and a warm rush in her heart. An owl flew over the gate and into her heart garden, then a falcon. Behind the two women stood a huge woman goddess. She was at least nine feet tall. She stood with her ram, and a distaff filled with flax. A heron settled on the fence beside the goddess. Her dress shimmered like water, a silvery gray.

"Mother Frigg . . . Welcome," Randine whispered. She bowed to her in her heart.

Frigg was silent and bowed her head in acknowl-edgement. Then she said to Randine, "May we come in?"

Randine bowed to the entourage inside and whis-pered, "Yes!"

They entered the gate, and Randine felt their pres-ence and power come to her, yet she felt her own power, too. Without speaking, Frigg pointed to the stream, and then showed what was needed. Randine was to be baptized in the falls by the two of her mentors, her elders. She saw the three of them standing naked, holding Randine arm in arm under the force of the water. They were to call on all the Goddesses in the baptism to cleanse her, and prepare her for her travels to Laerdal. The picture faded and Randine stood alone again inside her heart, with her wolf at her side and the owl overhead in a birch tree.

When she opened her eyes, the two older women were stretching their legs. She sat there a moment. Then in silence she stood up and began unhooking her blouse.

Ursula turned to her and without saying a word, walked towards her, reached into the basket and brought out a second small sack. Randine noticed the sack was white with blue bleeding through. It was the same sack Ursula had used when Randine was giving birth. The blue was woad, a chalk used for the symbol of Odin, the color for initiation.

Lena also began to undress. After Ursula had laid what they would need on a slab of stone in a neat fashion, she tossed a few herbs into the fire, and watched the smoke curl. Then Ursula undressed, too. Nothing was spoken. The only sound was the thunder of the falls and the trickle of water.

Lena guided Randine to a small stone altar. Randine could see the signs of Odin and Frigg carved above the altar in the stone cave wall. On the slab of stone, Ursula had laid all of the herbs and implements they would need. Ursula laid down the circle with the equidistant cross in the middle, and around it she placed a strand of flax, a large blue heron feather and a shell.

Randine had not seen women naked before, so it seemed odd in a way to witness their natural bodies. But as they moved around each other, soon it seemed as natural as anything. Their clothes seemed restrictive and stiff by comparison.

Ursula took the shell from the altar and scooped up some coals from the fire. Then she placed the dried sage and lavender flowers over the coals. She took the heron feather and motioned to Randine to stand back a bit from the altar so they could pass the smoking shell back and forth around her. First Lena and Ursula smoked each other then Randine. The shell was placed back on the altar.

Ursula took the woad and drew symbols on Randine's back—the symbols of Frigg and Odin for protection. She drew a line from each symbol down the center of her back that split at her hips and continued each line down Randine's legs to her feet. There below her navel, Ursula drew a spiral. Then she drew a line from the spiral that went up to her belly where she drew another spiral just where her ribs came together. Lena pulled Randine's hair back from her face, and held it there while Ursula continued to draw the line between her breasts. Then she drew a circle at the heart level, with a heart in the middle of it. Intersecting lines extended out from the four directions symbolizing the heart in the middle of life. Ursula drew a line across each breast to make two medicine circles. These lines continued under each arm to connect with the symbols on her back. The line from the middle of her chest at the medicine heart circle was continued up to her throat, and around in another spiral, then over the middle of her chin and to her mouth, and nose and to her forehead, where Ursula drew an eye. Lena parted her thick auburn hair down the middle, so the line could continue to the top of her head, where Ursula drew a medicine wheel in her thick auburn hair, then down the back of her neck and connect to the other line at her shoulders.

Randine had kept her eyes closed through the whole process. Now she opened them and looked at her blue and white body. The wheels of life were her breasts, the spirals her belly and womb. Her heart was the center of all. After drawing the spirals and circles on each other's faces, Lena and Ursula stood on either side of Randine and Lena spoke.

"Odin, Freya, Frigg, we honor you, as we honor the other gods. Thor and Freyja, Tyr and Iduna, Hella and Holda, Frey and Niord, Nethus, Heimdal and Uller, Loki, Skadi, Eir, Vor and Var, Jesus Christ, God and Goddess all from the living Sun, we present you your daughter Randine Hakonsdatter Stokanes Luster, daughter of Frigg and Odin, she comes to take up her work and her power. We, her midwives, Lena Petersdatter Erickson and Ursula Larsdatter Strøm, give her to you, as she is ready. Today she becomes the goddess as we are your daughters."

Lena completed the invocation and took a small cup from under the stones that Randine had not noticed before. It was full of milk, a second one was filled with beer, and a third one of honey. All were taken out of hiding. Lena and Ursula each took a cup and set the honey down on the altar. It was in a sugar bowl with two handles. First Ursula poured the beer over her head. "Blessed be the fruit of labor, of toil and of strength of men and women. Blessings on the maiden." Then Lena poured the milk over Randine's head.

"Blessed be the mother of all. Blessed be the Goddess who brings life, and the seed of men who gives it," Lena said.

Then they both picked up the small cup of honey, a handle for each of them, from the altar and slowly poured the honey over Randine. It dripped down her crown in all directions mixing with her thick beautiful auburn hair. She felt it drip down her face. Inside, she could feel a bolt of light enter her crown just as the honey touched her head. The lightening streak raced down inside her body and along her skin to her womb and through her legs, following the lines they had drawn down each leg to her feet and into the Earth. Her knees buckled slightly. Lena put her arm behind her to steady her. Randine gained her stance again, and felt the ecstatic light surging through her. Every nerve was tingling. She felt her nipples become erect and her labia were flushed and aroused and full of sacred light at the same time. She felt the waterfall of light enter her and move through her. It was as though all her circuits had been ignited.

"Blessed is the Crone, whose wisdom guides us. Maiden, Mother and Crone," Lena said.

"Let it move through you, do not hold on to it, Randine, just feel the pleasure and pain of the Goddess," Ursula whispered.

Randine felt a snake of light surging through her from her spine up her back, around the top of her head, and down to her heart and around to her womb again in a circuit. As it raced around, she felt the pain of loss and the opening of joy bursting through her. She felt the trickle of tears from her eyes making rivers.

As the electricity subsided, she felt the gentle touch of her elders on either side of her taking her arms. She opened her eyes and found that they were taking her to the waterfall. First they stepped before the fire and bowed, and then stepped into the trickling stream that ran down the center of the cave. The bottom of the stream was sandy with rocks here and there. As they took the steps towards the falls, Lena and Ursula sang a song that rose from inside of them.

Oh Goddess Goddess you are here, Great Mother, Great Father

Bless your Daughter,

Oh Goddess Goddess you are here, Great Mother, Great Father

Bless your Daughter.

Randine did not feel her feet on the rock nor her body, only the sudden shock of fresh water was over her, and over each of her friends. She gasped as they held on to her arms tightly now. She was engulfed in water, filled with cool blue light. For a moment she was one with everything, her feet on the rocks, her body covered in the falls. Lena and Ursula were with her, the light was moving in, around

her and through her. Then they stepped back and again
they plunged her into the sheets of water. Three times she
was blessed as they chanted. She became one with the cave,
with the light streaming through, with the water falling.

As they finished their song and ritual chanting, they
guided her back a few steps. The sun broke through the
clouds and streamed into the falling water with rainbows
dancing through the sheets of water. They all were stunned
at the beauty of the Goddess.

Randine felt her body pulse with life. As they guided
her back to the altar, they released her arms and knelt on
the floor of the cave, the sun was lower in the sky, shining
into the cave and lighting it up. Rainbows of light danced
through the falls and lit up the cave with dazzling color.

They bowed to the altar and Randine noticed that
there was no more blue woad on anyone. The honey, milk,
and beer had all washed away. The altar was the same as it
was, though it seemed more sacred to her now. The three
empty cups sitting there. She felt her forehead touch the
stone floor.

Ursula picked up the flax on the altar glowing in the
sunlight as it streamed in. Randine noticed it was woven,
and made it into a necklace. In the center was a Wheel of
life, and on either side, tied into the threads were the stones
of each of the four directions: an indigo blue one for Odin,
a silver one for Frigg, a green one for Freyja, a red one for
Thor.

Lena and Ursula took either side of the necklace and
put it over Randine's head. She bowed her head as they
slowly lowered the necklace over her. The symbol of the
wheel of life landed over her heart.

"Wear this in remembrance of this day. Know that
though it is just a symbol, through it, you can gain the wisdom you need inside your own heart, wherever you go. You
will never be lost if you wear it."

She could see Lena and Ursula had tears streaming
down their faces. Then each woman hugged her. The three

of them stood together holding hands.

"Thank you Gods and Goddesses for being here with Randine, who is one of us now. Blessed Be." Lena stepped back and dropped Randine's hand.

"Blessed Be." Ursula stepped back too and released her other hand.

Randine stood there for a moment watching the light play across the altar and feeling it pulse through her.

The ritual was over.

"Blessed be," Randine heard herself say.

Slowly Ursula opened the four directions along with the earth, sky and center, by giving thanks to Frigg and Odin, and all the Gods and Goddesses, she too said, "It is done." The three women dried themselves and put their clothes back on. They collected the remaining things off the altar. The last of the coals had burned out, and they washed the place where they had built the fire with water from the stream. Lena had supplied the wooden bucket for this use a few days before the ritual. She had also brought down the items they used for the ritual, so they did not have to bring it with Randine.

They placed a bit of the flat bread and other food items on the altar in gratitude. Then they ate what was left and celebrated each bite, as rituals always make everyone hungry. When they were finished, they took the bits of food from the altar and placed them in the waterfall.

One by one, they stepped back through the falls, this time from the left side of the waterfall. Randine now realized that there was a trail on that side that led to a huge slab of rock that protected them from falling mist. This is how the two women had come into the cave. It was another entrance to the cave that opened downstream a ways.

They walked all the way to the fork in the trail, and all the way back to Bergen, not saying a thing. When they reached the hustle and bustle of the streets, they walked side by side, with Randine between them. Her hair was mostly dried by the time she reached the edge of town. Randine had never felt so new.

Ursula's little house stood there as it had before. But this time Randine noticed more closely the wheel of life, or Celtic cross, carved in the rafters over the door-frame that meant more to her now then ever before. She touched it as she entered and bowed her head just a bit as she ducked inside.

The Vikings had danced around this symbol, so had all the settlers of the British Isles, all the way to Ireland and beyond. Some say it was the symbol for a balanced life before Christianity came and changed everything. They saw the value of love of the Christ in the center of the wheel as the heart of love that is in each one of us. 'Someday perhaps people will see that the two ways work together,' Randine thought.

Her mother was sitting with Henrik in the rocker. He was awake playing with a toy bear. When he saw Randine, his face burst with light. The same light Randine had felt inside the cave.

"Mama, Mama," Henrik cried out. Randine was glowing with love.

Chapter Thirteen
Goodbye to Bergen

Monday, 28 July 1823
Randine's Diary
Today is the day my life in Bergen ends, and my new life begins. Who knows what will happen in Laerdal? The adventure is exciting. I am glad to leave Bergen behind, though I will miss Ursula and Lena, that is for sure...

"It is time," she said out loud, as she surveyed what she had to pack. "I am ready now." Randine's clothes and belongings were laid out on the bed. 'There isn't much after all, not that anyone in Norway has much to their name,' Randine thought as she remembered the houses she had been in and how basically people lived.

There was her bünd, or traditional dress; a second skirt, a blouse, and cap; socks, two pair; a button hook for her shoes. That is more than most have, she thought. She also packed underwear, a long winter undershirt with sleeves that went on under her blouse, a wool under-slip for winter, and her underpants that she wore with a rag when she was bleeding, though she was not nursing except at night for comfort with Henrik. She brought a broach and some earrings that her mother had given her, her hairbrush, three combs for her hair made of tortoise shell, and her rune stones. She couldn't forget them. They would help her find her way in her new world. She couldn't forget her apron that she wore when she cooked and visited the women in labor.

She would have to make more mittens this winter, and some for Henrik, too. She placed them in her carpetbag, along with wooden needles for knitting, setting aside her hair-brush and Henrik's tiny socks, extra pants, and a shirt for him; all these items would remain on top so she could get to them easily. She thought of her belongings at her parents' home, how her wardrobe was full of things she rarely wore.

Deep inside the bag were Henrik's good wool clothes for winter and special occasions; otherwise, he was ready with what he had on, plus a bib or two. That should do it. His diapers were in a separate bag already downstairs. But soon he would be trained to use the latrine or pee in the bushes. Ola could help him with that.

She looked around the dark attic where she had lived now almost two years; it had become home. Soon she would be cleaning out her own house, and have her own little cabin to take care of once she arrived in Laerdal, she thought.

After two long years, Ola came back from sea for good and was finally getting transferred to his hometown of Laerdal. He had been in and out of Bergen from time to time. He would still have to go sailing from Bergen, but the papers were in to transfer to the Army but that might be a few years more when he was officially transferred to the Army. This gave him the time he needed to be with his family and take care of his duties in his home territory once they had finished the harvest.

Ola would meet them at the carriage house. He would escort her and Henrik to Laerdal and he could take the time he needed to get Randine and Henrik settled this summer. Eventually he would be stationed in Laerdal permanently.

In some ways, Randine was glad to be leaving Bergen to begin a new life, even if it meant adjusting to a new community. It was Henrik's father's home after all. As a wet nurse, she would be treated well for the sacrifice she was making, giving her life to care for this tiny boy who needed a mother.

Anna and Haagen were moving with them back to her mother's home in Sogndal just down the fjord from

Laerdal. Father had made a nice living as a merchant. Now they could live comfortably in Sogndal and not have to worry about their survival: a rare thing in Norway. Her father was from Årdal, a small community not far from Laerdal. The villages had summer festivals together most years. She had heard stories from her father since she was a tiny girl about the fjords and the festivals. How people traveled by rowboat from town to town down the long finger of seawater with mountains on either side. How life there was different, more quiet, and the people steadfast. The majestic mountains and harsh life molded the people's spirits and made their emotional waters seem deeper, though indeed the fjords themselves were deep, almost as deep as the mountains were high. You could not see the tops sometimes, and you could not see the dark bottom. The people of this land had to be like the mountains and the water to survive, strong and resilient. Father talked of how hard people worked on the farms for survival. How the people worked together to store and put up food for the long winter months. Their communities were solid and stable, and had been that way for a thousand years, even though they were poor and death was a constant companion. They were slow to change—the challenge would be feeling a part in such a remote farming community with people so set in their ways.

Randine brushed aside her worried thoughts. No one would question her integrity or ask too many questions of her own fate prior to coming to Laerdal. She also had been an apprentice to Ursula for the last two years; this would be long enough to present herself to the church as a midwife. She could further help the people, and prove herself to them. Never mind that she was from Bergen. People will be curious. That is for sure.

"Ursula are you down there?" Randine whispered from the loft.

"Yes, yes, are you ready?" Ursula looked up around the ladder as Randine looked down from the loft.

"Ya, I am, here is my bag." Randine hoisted the bag from the bed to the ladder and eased it down to Ursula's waiting hands. As she caught it she whispered back,

"Anything else?" Ursula asks.

"Yes, I have something for you." Randine turned around and placed her foot on the familiar rung on the loft ladder and lowered herself step by step. She took a final look inside the loft, knowing it was unlikely that she would return. She might never see Ursula again either, as she reached the floor below with her foot. Ursula was standing with her hands folded over her belly. Randine embraced her.

"I am so sad to leave you and all we have had together Ursula. I have this for you."

Randine reached into her blouse and pulled out a poem she had written to Ursula after her initiation. "Please open it after I leave."

"There, there." Ursula took the envelope and hugged her tight and patted her on the back.

"We always knew it was temporary; you were here until it was time for the next step, isn't that right?" Ursula took Randine by the shoulders and looked her straight in the eye. Tears were spilling everywhere for Randine. Ursula's eyes were moist too.

"Dry your tears my dear, we can always write to each other." Ursula pulled out her handkerchief from her skirt pocket. "Who knows, I might take a trip to Laerdal sometime. Or if you go to Christiania, you have to pass through Bergen. Come now, Randine, we shall see each other again, I promise you this much."

"You have been a rock for me Ursula. Thank you for, for everything."

Randine managed a smile. Henrik began to stir as the two women embraced again, and Randine blew her nose in Ursula's handkerchief. Ursula dried Randine's eyes, and Randine tried to put a smile on her face for Henrik. Randine stuffed the handkerchief into her pocket absentmindedly.

"There, there, sweet boy." Randine smothered him in kisses until he sleepily woke and cuddled under her chin.

"Okay, time to go," Ursula said efficiently. "Oh here is my letter of introduction to the minister. You will need it when you arrive."

Randine nodded a thank you, and took the letter and slipped it into her carpetbag. She checked Henrik's pants; they were only slightly damp. Not wet enough to change him yet.

Ursula picked up the bags, the diaper bag, and the carpetbag, with her money purse clipped to her belt. She placed her cap on her head and opened the door for Randine and sleepy Henrik. 'Soon we will be in the carriage, on our way to Laerdal, and then, who knows?' Randine thought.

As Ursula and Randine made their way down the cobblestone street to the harbor, they offered a bow at the waist to the people they met along the way. Because they had helped so many women, often they were stopped and thanked profusely. Then as a courtesy, Randine and Ursula asked questions of them about the children and the mother. Henrik was lowered to the ground from Randine's arms at those times, and he would cling to her skirt and hide between her legs. Then when the conversation was over, they would say their good-byes, and Randine would pick him up again. Ursula would switch hands with the bags, and they would get another few feet before they met someone else.

Soon they could see the harbor and the sails of the tall ships. The Bergen port always looked majestic as they started down the hill, especially when the sun was out. Today it was sunny, a rare day in Bergen.

"Look Henrik, there is your Papa's ship!" Randine exclaimed, pointing to it. He turned in her arms to look at the boats and squeaked out an excited, "Bo, Bo, Pa, Pa!"

They could see the wider harbor with the carriage house on the dock of the harbor and her parents waiting together at the dock standing by the carriage that would take them to Gudvagen. Lena and Peter Erickson met them coming down the hillside and walked them to the harbor to meet Ola and her parents. They were all traveling together, Randine, her parents and Henrik and Ola. Ola was not there as yet, though she knew he was nearby. His ship was in after all. She felt nervous to see him again.

As the others bowed and greeted Anna and Haagen, Randine put Henrik down for a moment and hugged both of her parents. She began to cry again and reached in her pocket for her handkerchief and took out Ursula's.

"Keep it dear, it is a reminder to you that I am always here for you." Ursula thought it a good time to reveal her going away gift to Randine. "Here dear, is a pot of lavender for you. It will help the women of Laerdal. I have wrapped the plant in earth inside a sack to carry, so it will last the journey. Plant it on the south side of your home, and it will grow in the sun, protected from the weather."

Randine dropped her hands and took the small sack from Ursula. Then she threw her arms around Ursula and whispered to her mentor, "Oh Ursula, I will miss you the most. Thank you for all your teachings, thank you for your love."

Ursula began to weep too, which was unusual for her. "I love you too Randine, and remember, I will always return your letters, if you write."

Just then Ola came running up to them, bowing rapidly to all he met in the departure group. He scooped up Henrik and tickled him.

Before Ola had the proper time to greet anyone, Haagen took charge.

"Time to go, the carriage is waiting to take us to the ferry at Gudvagen. Randine! Mother! Let's go."

Ola nodded, "One moment, please, I must say goodbye to my mates."

He turned on his heels carrying Henrik with him and walked briskly to the group of sailors several meters away near the dock. After saying goodbye to his comrades, and showing them his son, he shifted his feet as he said good-bye to his Captain and crew members. He saluted his captain and then his mates. Henrik saluted too. Everyone chuckled as he turned quickly to get on board the carriage.

Randine hugged Lena and Peter and gave them a small gift she had bought with some of the money she made as a midwife. It was a box, carved by a neighbor. The top was painted with rosemaling patterns in blue, red, and green. Lena was dabbing her eyes with her handkerchief.

"It is so lovely, thank you. How thoughtful of you Randine. Have a good trip dear. We will miss you so. Take good care of little Henrik."

Just then, Erica came running down the hill as fast as she could manage; at eight months pregnant she was quite a sight.

"Wait! Randine, Randine, I have something for you." Erica caught Randine's arm as she was about to pull herself up into the carriage. Henrik, ahead of her, had settled into his grandmother's lap.

"I made this with Mrs. E's help." Erica held up a small sweater for Henrik made with handspun yarn that she had spun herself. She could tell it was a first go, but Randine didn't mind. She let go of the wagon for a moment to take the sweater in both hands.

"Oh, how lovely it is Erica! Thank you, he will need it this winter. Good bye, dear Erica." Randine hugged Erica with both arms still holding the sweater. She thought of how lucky she was compared to her. Erica has to make her way with a child in tow, with no husband. She will always be labeled as a woman of ill repute. Unless she finds a man to marry her, her chances of every being more than a maid and a mistress are very slim.

Ola was behind Erica when Randine let go; he stepped in to help her up. His touch was gentle and efficient. He latched the carriage door behind her without looking at her, then swung himself up onto the front seat of the wagon to sit with the driver.

The carriage was open to the sky; there was a canopy to cover them if it rained. The canopy rested on the back of Randine's seat separating the seats and the luggage as the bags and belongings were in the back of the wagon. Two bench seats faced each other. Anna, Haagen and Henrik rested on one seat facing the back of the carriage. They had the last glimpses of Bergen. Randine sat beside their lunch basket on the other bench facing the front, heading into the future. She looked back out of the carriage to her friends, knowing she may not see some of them ever again.

"Good-bye, God Bless, Godspeed!" they shouted and waved to the travelers.

"Good-bye, take good care!" Randine shouted back to them and waved.

"Everybody ready! Next stop Gudvagen!" said the driver in his sing-song voice, as he snapped his whip above the horses.

She turned around to view what was ahead. The carriage driver, Pal Tomasson, and Ola had their backs to the passengers. She was glad she was facing front. She could study Ola as he chatted away with the driver.

Ursula turned toward home, and read Randine's message as she slowly walked up the street back to her home.

Arrival

for Ursula
Born in a thunderstorm,
hail crashing,
lightning bolting all around,
My mother, the sea,
carried my little coracle
to the other side,
to the other side of her
broad thigh, to the other
side of the sea.

Family on both sides stood around,

stood around the shore
and I swam to Father's arms,
to Odin's arms,
as he was hovering overhead,
hovering overhead.

And he said to me, My daughter,
my darling daughter, dear,
you shall be the one, the one, the one,
you shall be the one to carry on.
Your heart the sail, your body
the boat, your spirit will blow
your craft to inland shores,

And I will be there for you,
oh darling child, darling child
dear, and I will be there to carry
you as you carry those you serve,
as you carry those you serve.

Ursula our midwife washed me,
my mother wrapped me,
and soon I was on my way,
how initiation flashes
and destiny dashes us, as we shape
our lives from foam, as
our lives are shaped from foam.

Before I started on my way
I could hear my father's echoing
as I stood on solid ground,
solid ground, solid ground,

Be not afraid of anything
as you shall always know,
you are being carried along,
carried along, carried along
You will be carried along
to where your destiny roams.

Chapter Fourteen
On to Laerdal

Monday, 28 July 1823

Randine's Diary

Dear Diary, Today I leave Bergen for good. What will I do without Ursula? She has been the mother I wish I had...

It was late July, and there was a warm wind blowing off the mountains beckoning them to Laerdal. The carriage lurched forward with an awkward lunge. Randine's tears kept flowing as her thoughts raced for a moment when she thought of the people she would miss in Bergen. Her whole life had been lived there. She felt the tug in her heart as James's memory stayed by the sea. She had not realized what a hold the sea had on her in remembering him— as they left she felt the memories tear away like a membrane at birth. Yes, she was leaving the womb of Bergen for another journey. Her tears were the birthing waters. All of these memories rushed back in a huge swirl, kicked up like the dust from the horse's hooves.

As Bergen faded from view and farms began to appear along the roads, Randine was realizing that she had never been out of Bergen! A rush of excitement for the new adventures suddenly flooded her as her curiosity overtook her sadness.

Ola was chatting with the driver. Randine's mother and father were watching their Bergen community, where they had lived for several decades, recede behind them. They were leaving their son's burial site, their friends, their church. At the same time both of them were looking forward to settling again into life in Sogndal. Henrik had been asleep in his grandmother's arms since they left Bergen, with the gentle sway of carriage and clip clop rhythm of horses. The road slowly curved away into the mountains.

After they had settled into the journey and had travelled in the countryside for a while, Randine asked,

"Mother, tell me about Sogndal. What can you say? Are the people all farmers, what do they do to eat? Are there celebrations for harvest? Tell me about your parents, you never speak of them."

"So many questions at once, dear." Anna shifted the sleeping Henrik in her arms. "Well, it is a small town, the whole town about as big as the Bergen port, plus a few streets of houses around the dock. That is all."

"But what of the land?" Randine asked.

Haagen added. "Mountains rise behind the town with only a footpath or two rising to mountain pastures. There is a water passage to get to Sogndal as it faces southwest, but is hidden from the harsh winter winds by the steep mountains on the west side of the fjord, and the sun comes up over one ridge in the mornings and shines down one branch of the fjord and makes the water sparkle. The land is not too steep so there is some farming. But then the mountains are right there a short way from town on the west and there are few places left to build unless you go higher up the mountain to the upper pastures."

Anna continued, "The mountains are steep to the west, and lower in the east, so mountains are all around on three sides with a narrow pass that goes to Laerdal. We get a nice sunset when you live east in town looking down the finger of fjord that brings the boats from the west. A few homes near the top of the mountain outside the village can see the last rays of sun that are put out by the snow cap across the fjord. There is a market on Saturdays, and the store, and a church. The boys and some girls whose parents send them to the church are taught letters and numbers by the minister." Anna's description trailed off as she became lost in memory.

Haagen added, "Of course the town is facing the water and a sturdy dock greets all the boats. People fish and farm, where they can, though there is not much land for big farms, most are small. Everyone has a garden. Some farms are high, where the mountains have mercy, and in the summer young boys take the sheep even higher where there is more for them to eat," Haagen paused. "Life is slower there, Randine. People live and die with the seasons. It is the same, I think in Laerdal," her father added. "Isn't that right Ola?"

Ola turned around slightly, "Yes sir, it is the same, though Laerdal has more land. The valley runs north and south with somewhat steeper slopes than Sogndal and takes a dog-leg turn from the fjord where the town is, so the sun warms the village well in summer and the western slope too to some extent. The Lysne farms are located near the end of the valley where the light is, Lysne mean light, the land where the light is. It is our address as well as our name. Flowers and farms string along and it tends to be kept warm by the river that runs all year. It is very beautiful. Have you been there Mrs. Stokanes?"

"Yes, the two villages had festivals together when I was younger; one year in Sogndal, the next year in Laerdal. Many friends and family would visit during spring and summer—that is, until the festivals begin at the end of September. Then we would have several days, and people would come out of the mountains to celebrate with their neighbors at the harvest festival. At the end of the harvest celebrations, as they went on for days, we would say good-bye to them for the winter and to our friends in Laerdal, until spring planting in May. In late autumn, though, as the harvest was done, the slaughtering took place in November, "blood month" we called it, you know for the blood moon. People were too busy, putting up food, and preparing their winter stores to socialize much. Of course Christmas was always celebrated with family in our own villages for weeks. Winter is a resting time, time to repair our sleds and reins and equipment for the men, and women spun yarn, knitted and sewed and repaired clothes. But then in spring we would see again whoever survived the winter and we began a new planting season." Anna smiled at her fond memories."It is a good life, harder than Bergen in most ways, but a good life."

"Then there is the May festival when the seeds are planted and the dancing and mating take place!" Haagen chuckled and Anna gave him an elbow.

Randine laughed as she watched Ola's reaction. Ola turned back around and looked up and out of the carriage at the trees and landscape. Randine noticed he seemed distant this morning and barely looked at Randine and she was just deciding whether she was going to put up with this behavior or not. Then she blurted out.

"Ola, are the people in Laerdal *all* your family?"

Ola was startled at her question, as she had not spoken directly since he last left Ursula's house several weeks before. He had not really greeted her properly at the harbor when they boarded the carriage, and Randine was a little angry with him for this. Her words poked him a bit, as they were intended to do.

"No, no not all." He looked at her briefly with a raised eyebrow, then turned back to the road, his eyes focused ahead.

"What are the other family names?" Randine persisted.

Ola took a breath and then began to speak slowly, looking up in his brow still avoiding her glare, then glancing briefly at her half-turning around, wondering why she wanted to know so much all of a sudden.

"There are the Moes by the river, and the Larsens in town, who own the store and a small boarding house. There are many cotter families who help with the farms, and more Tomasson Knudsons by the river's mouth. The Bø, or farm, carries no one's last name, as it is where newlyweds and cotters live when they need extra housing. Most families are named after the piece of land they live on, especially farmers. That is why our name, Lysne, or light, gives our address on the Lysne farms. Everyone knows where we live by the fact that there is more light there than any other farm in the valley. There are many different families in Laerdal. You will see." He finished so she would not ask more, and turned again to the road as if his eyes were needed for the driver to see.

The day went by quickly and everything was so new to Randine. The farms and houses were different from the houses in Bergen. Most houses in Bergen were painted white, with black tile roofs; here the houses were often red or painted different colors with white trim and black wooden shingles on roof.

"This farm is the one where we have gotten good pork," her father pointed out. "They bring it to Bergen, only a half-day by carriage."

Henrik woke up as he heard the talking, and she asked the driver to stop so they could stop for lunch. They were half way to Gudvagen and the sun was straight up in the sky. Anna passed Henrik to Randine, took the food basket from the seat, and stepped out of the carriage with Haagen's helping hand. Ola jumped off the seat where he was sitting with the driver and untied another basket where the trunks and bags were kept at the back of the carriage. Ola and Haagen took the baskets and spread a cloth resting on the top of one basket out under the tree for all to sit. Randine changed Henrik's diaper in the carriage while the driver looked after the horses.

Anna unpacked the food: some cheese wrapped in a cloth, bread, a bit of sausage that Randine had cooked that morning, and some milk in a bottle. The loaf of bread was fresh and perfect for the sandwiches they would make. Randine called to Ola to help her and Henrik out of the carriage. Randine handed the round loaf to Ola to cut slices.

The driver, Pal, joined everyone after he tended the horses. He unhitched them from the wagon, and took them to the stream that ran along the road to water them. Then he tied their lines to a tree so they would not run ahead.

Pal was going home to Gudvagen, and the horses knew it as they had not wanted to stop. He was from Gudvagen. His uncle ran the ferryboats.

After lunch Randine packed the leftover food in the basket. She chased Henrik around the tree they had lunch under. He loved being free from the carriage. He had gone from walking to running in a very short time, and now he ran whenever he could. He jumped onto Ola's broad back. Always, Henrik broke the ice between Randine and Ola.

"OHHH a sea monster, I think." Ola said grabbing his son on his back with one arm. Henrik squealed with laughter as Randine stood there watching. She laughed at Ola's surprise.

"He is like you I think, Ola, but be careful, I don't want him to spit up his lunch," Randine said softly. Ola turned to see Randine smiling at him. He picked up the boy, stood up and brought him over to her upside down.

"He laughs like you Randine," Ola said, looking deeply into her blue eyes, and for the first time, something more was there than this agreement they had for her to come to Laerdal to take care of Henrik. Randine took her charge, and looked back at Ola squarely.

"Ola, we need to talk before we get to Laerdal," Randine said, surprising him. "Maybe mother can watch Henrik for a while when we get to the boat."

"Al-right, yes, I think it would be good," Ola replied reluctantly. "I, I have some things to say to you too, Randine, I-I want to...."

"Time to go," Haagen interrupted for a second time. "We must get to the launch before dark."

Randine turned with Henrik squirming in her arms and let him down to run to the carriage. The ride was easier after that. Ola was less stiff, and Randine's request seemed to relax him, though he hardly spoke.

She remembered Ursula's words. "You must set your requirements, and things will unfold. You will see."

Through the long carriage ride most of the travelers

were silent and some slept. When they reached the dock
at Gudvagen, Randine was surprised to see that there were
just a few buildings, the ferry man's home with a few out
buildings, and a small plot of earth that was freshly tilled.
If you didn't know this was a ferry dock, you could miss it.
Randine noticed a small building that looked like an out-
house at the end of the dock. This is where tickets were
sold. A small sign rested above it, "Gudvagen." Ola pointed
out the ferryboat rowers moving towards them from down
the fjord.

"Each boat holds four passengers with two rowers,
six in all," Ola explained. "If there are any strong men on
board, they take turns with the hired oarsman. It is a thirty-
five miles of steady rowing to Laerdal. It will take us all day
at a good clip. We will rest tonight in the cabin, and leave in
the morning."

According to Haagen's map, the Sognfjord was the
largest such waterway in Norway. Ocean water stretches
150 miles into the heart of Norway's southern spoon. Many
small towns and isolated farms were dotted along the
banks, with water their only transport. There were some
roads, especially from Laerdal, where the land was more
forgiving, and the vise of the mountains was less severe
than here at Gudvagen. A single mail route connected
Laerdal to Bjøkum and Borgund and eventually Christiania.
That was the only road to the east.

There were two other ways to get to Laerdal, one by
boat from the mouth of the Sognfjord, and the other by boat
from Gudvagen. Gudvagen was on one of the many fingers
of the fjord that stretched like a clawed hand from the
base of the mountains, and had built up some earth at the
streams base over the centuries. One could not see the top
of the mountains from the water, except from a distance. It
was a shorter and less strenuous trip from Gudvagen than
down the other fork from Bergen to Laerdal.

Randine was in awe of the beauty of Gudvagen. The
mountains along the fjord rose straight up thousands of

feet, with few level places anywhere in sight. Some farms clung to an open green place around a bend or between mountain peaks where a stream ran. As the sun was setting, the light reflected the mountain's twin in the water. The air was clear yet with a slight fog settling over the water. There was a stillness here that she had never experienced between cries of the Seagulls. It hung in the air everywhere. You could not see where the water went, once it reached the end where the mountain showed its twin in the water. 'One would have to know the way through the fjords or you could be lost forever,' Randine thought.

"Have you heard about the ice children of Angrboda, Randine?" Haagen asked as he and Ola unloaded the carriage.

"No father I haven't. Tell me," Randine replied. Anna was tending to Henrik.

"Well, Angrboda is the ice queen who lives at the top of the mountain. Her consort was Loki with whom she had three children; a wolf named Fenrir, a serpent Jormungand, and a daughter named Hel. Now Odin, the war god, out of fear, banished the daughter to the world beneath the worlds, to the place of the unglorious dead. It was a terrible place, I dare say. Jormungand was banished into the ocean. It is said he lives at the bottom of the fjord. Now in summer and winter, Jormungand and Hel can be seen by their mother, but can never embrace. That is why the reflections are so clear and strong in these fjords. Once a year she breathes her cold breath down the mountain. It lasts for nine months of autumn, winter and spring, in revenge for her children."

"And what happened to Fenrir, the wolf?" She wanted to know.

"Fenrir was taken by Odin to Asgård, you know we call it heaven today. There, in Asgård, he was tied up on a magic tether, so that he would not tear apart the Gods," Randine's father Haagen said solemnly. "But he did break loose eventually and he escaped, and all was destroyed. That is when the Christians came to Norway."

"Now Haagen stop, enough of your stories! Come let us get our luggage to the boat," Anna admonished.

Haagen leaned towards his daughter, "You ask the ferryman if we are to leave tonight. Not on your life! He will say, Jormungand raises his head to find his mother then! You ask him." Haagen whispered to the two of them, winking at Ola. Randine playfully pushed her father away, laughing.

"Father, you used to scare me with other tales as a child. I am glad Henrik is too young to understand. He would be scared too, and we would be up all night with him." She laughed.

"Henrik has little fear, he is mostly joy, I think," Haagen said, chuckling.

"Ya," Ola said. "He is so playful ... pure joy."

The boatmen helped the family with their things, and then announced that they would be leaving first thing in the morning. Randine laughed and her father grinned then became serious again.

"Jormungand, what did I tell you." Haagen seemed so serious the boatman looked hard at Haagen until he saw the glint in his eye. Then the boatman said slowly,
"Ya, we let Jormungand rest at night. No sense in stirring the waters. We have a nasty troll who lives at the end of the bend who would take passage from us, or want a child instead. So we wait."

Ola and Randine looked at each other and smiled. Then the boatman said with glee, "Ah, these young people don't believe us. But you tell them, Sir, we have many stories and tales to entertain us along the Sognfjord. They are alive in these grand mountains, are they not?"

"Ya, you betcha." Haagen smiled, patting the boatman's back.

After their things were tied into the hold of the small boats, Randine and Ola and her family took lodging at a long house built just for visitors. They entered in the center of the building, and were greeted by the sight of a long table and seating area with Pal's aunt Gretchen greeting them with the fireplace on the far wall. The beds were built-in walls around the room, with men on one end, women at the other. The seating area around the broad fireplace stretched across the middle of the room. The seating appeared to be already arranged for conversation with other passengers. The night's lodging was part of the fare. For a few extra skillings the ferryman's wife and daughters served dinner. Everyone had fun telling stories and laughing at the tales that went on late into the evening.

While the stories were beginning to be told and after Henrik was bedded down, Ola tapped Randine's shoulder and nodded towards the door.

"Good night, ladies and gentleman, we are going to get some air," Ola said courteously. "Good night, good rest," the chorus of voices sang together.

They slipped outside to take an evening stroll. Pausing beneath the trees, they could hear wolves howling in the mountains, and the water slightly lapping against the rocky shore. The moon shone on the water as if it were made of glass.

"I am glad you asked to talk, Randine, we have scarcely had a chance since we made our agreement to come to Laerdal," Ola began cautiously. "There is much I want to say to you, and I have not yet found the words."

"Have you found them now?" Randine shot back more harshly than she meant to. "I am sorry Ola, sometimes I speak too harshly. What is it that you would like to tell me?"

"I think I have them now," Ola said slowly feeling more cautious.

"Randine, I will not hide the truth from you. You and I have no promises made. Officially you are Henrik's wet nurse-that is all. I am a sailor soon to be transferred to the Army if all goes well."

"Do you have other women Ola? Is that what you are saying?"

"No, that is not it...There are many women I have been with all over in many places. Not just in Bergen. It is part of being a sailor. But I do not love them, I do not have other children...but that is not what I wanted to talk about with you Randine." He looked upset.

"How do you know if you have other children?" Randine was not going to cut him any slack at this point.

"I am careful. Most of the prostitutes have some children. Then they go out of service."

"Service! You mean you sailors use them up, then they have to fend for themselves when they get pregnant!"

"Randine, it is not like that."

"Oh no? Not for you, that is for sure. Did you see that young girl at the harbor who gave Henrik the sweater? She is Erica, pregnant from one of your friends. Her parents abandoned her. So did he and now she is fourteen years old and left with a child. What is she to do once her child is born? How is she to make a living? She is not even a whore, Ola. She just fell in love—same as ...as anyone, as me, as you."

Randine was angry and she couldn't help herself, she had seen too much. There was so much hurt for these girls to bear that she bore with them. She could see his face soften in the moonlight, and she turned away from him to look at the moon rising over the water. She felt the tears rising up and out of her eyes. A silver moon shone through the black mountains and on the water; there were two moons, two mountains, two of everything reflected in the water.

"Randine please, that is not what I wanted to talk about." Ola stepped towards her and grabbed her by the shoulders.

"I love Henrik and I am glad you agreed to come with us. Why do you think I want to bring you to Laerdal? I want you to be with my family, until I can return there too."

Randine broke away walked a few steps down to the shore, then turned to face him. Her heart was ready to burst. "Why don't you come now Ola, leave the service, work for your brother on the farm? You could if you wanted to."

Randine was really crying now, she couldn't hold it in anymore. Surprising herself she stood there sobbing, cursing her tears, but did not hide her face. She wanted an answer. But she was also afraid for these sudden feelings she had for Ola, why would she demand that he come now? She did not love him.

Ola, looked down at his feet, shuffled and sighed, his hands in his pockets.

"I cannot come just yet. I don't make enough money. I have been in the service eleven years. One more year and I can switch service branches. I will have enough rank to be a sergeant in the Army if I transfer branches. When I have served for fifteen years, I can choose where I want to be based. I could come then to Laerdal. Five more after that and I will have a pension. Then I can buy a farm. That is why Randine, you will see me much more when we get to Laerdal than you could from Bergen. You will see how it is there. I love my brother, and would do anything for him, but I will not work under him like a cotter, unless I am working towards the goal of having my own place. This way, I have my freedom, I have my, my, manhood. It is not my fault that I am a second son."

Randine had not heard his explanation before of why he would not just come to Laerdal now.

"So this is why the wait? ... I see. I do not understand the service."

"You are only seventeen, Randine, I am twenty-seven. There is much difference in our ages. You are not old enough to understand how all this can work out. It will take time. For you to be my wife by Laerdal standards, in the farming class, you must be at least eighteen. I must save money for the wedding, for the feast. If I were just a cotter it would be different. Cotters marry at any age."

"Ola, I need to know. What are your intentions with me, not just with Henrik, I see those plainly, but with me?"

Randine felt herself hardening into a boulder. She was not going to budge. She handed him a rock with her words to see how he would swim with it.

Suddenly, Anna called to Randine. "Randine, dear, where are you?"

"Oh no," she sighed under her breath, then said loudly: "I am here with Ola, we are talking, I will be in soon. Mother please check on Henrik will you?" Randine was trying to sound calm and normal, but her mother could hear the tension in her voice.

"Dear are you alright?" Anna said from the door. "Do you have your shawl?"

"Yes, just go to bed. I will be there shortly," Randine said more quietly.

Ola looked at her face against the moonlight. He wondered if she saw on his face what he saw on hers. One side dark and one side light, like the halved moon itself. Randine wondered if he could see her pain, as she saw his. Could he see her love, as she was beginning to see his? They stood together like the goddess Hella and Thor the warrior. Just then, he reached for her hand, but dropped it suddenly. Then he turned away, and came back closer.

"Randine, I hope we will eventually marry. But you are so young, and I am not done with my work at sea. I have a two-year commitment that I must fulfill. As I said, in Laerdal, most women do not marry until they are at least eighteen, especially in the farming class—on the eighteenth birthday for women—we call it their wedding birthday. You won't be eighteen until November, so we could not marry anyway until next spring. However, I am committed until the following year. You see it is different in the country. That means at least two years before we could marry."

Randine felt scared of the future for the first time, and also confused. This was the first time they had spoken of what it was like in the country. What he was telling her was that a wedding for them would be at least another two to three years away. She would turn eighteen just before

Henrik's third birthday in November. They could not be be-trothed for another year until after her nineteenth birthday. Then he would not be done until the following year when she would be twenty.

"That, the eighteenth birthday, is when most girls get their bowl and spoon, not before. But with my orders the way they are, you cannot expect me to promise until I am sure. My orders could change, and then I could be in Trondheim or Christiania for a year or even two. They try to work with our farms, releasing us for the harvests, but I could not expect them to do what I would like so we could be together." Ola was being as plain as he could now. He paused and then added. "My brother and I are Christians and mother, too. My whole family is somewhat religious. The new preacher in Laerdal is much more rule-bound than the last. I have heard that his wife is rather high-minded. She is rather strict about morality. These rules, they come to protect the young women from birthing too soon. The preacher would not approve of you Randine. Neither would my brother, nor the preacher's wife, if they knew your age and your history. It is bad enough that I come with Henrik without his ...with a wet nurse rather than his real mother."

"I am all the mother he will ever need or know, Ola," Randine said as calmly as she could manage.

"Yes, I know this, I didn't mean ... Randine I am ex-plaining what it is like in the country."

Randine turned away from him and reached for Ursula's hanky and continued walking away from the lodge towards the dock. The broad end of the fjord looked like a lake in the moonlight, the dock tucked under the hill on the far side. Ola followed behind her slowly. As she walked, the pieces of Ola's explanation fell into place. She turned around to him.

"So your intention is for us to marry, Ola, when you return and get orders for the army post in Laerdal?"

"Yes, as soon as I have enough for a small house and the wedding feast, when you turn nineteen or twenty. I should be able to give you the bowl and spoon then. But if there is any hint that we have been intimate, we will be cast away from Laerdal, we could not stay there! It is too small, too strict, and traditional. You would be hurt the most, they might even put you in stocks."

"Stocks!" Randine said, shocked. She had never heard this before. But there was much she was learning about her new home. "Stocks! For what crime!?"

"For being a woman too young to have children, for being single without betrothal, for being unmarried, for being a harlot." Ola looked down away from her.

"Randine, Laerdal is a wonderful place, but gossip flies through town fast, from one end of the valley to the other, there is no need for a town crier."

Ola was dead serious. She could see he was only trying to protect her, Henrik and himself. Randine stopped at the dock and sat down on a pier that connected the dock to the shore.

"Ola, do you think I am a harlot?"

"No, of course not, you are no different than me, we fell in love with those we intended to marry and they both died. This is what is true. I know that you must have captured James's heart, as you have mine."

Randine looked into his eyes, and could see he was full of feeling for her. Randine's heart opened to him for the first time. He reached for her hand this time.

"Ola, thank you. I am glad to hear we might have a future together. Though we still need to know each other better and we have much to overcome from our losses. I am glad I am not just cast way in Laerdal and there is some intention here that might be more permanent." Her heart was so open with love for him suddenly. She felt the spirit of passion rising in her.

"Randine, I want you to be safe and unharmed." Ola reached for her other hand and she reached for his. Then he pulled her up from sitting and off the pier, and pressed her to him. He was like a wall of warmth, towering over her.

His arms were strong and huge wrapping around her small frame. Slowly she put her arms around him too, and held on to his waist. She felt his body soften, and hers too. They were an odd fit. She was so much smaller, yet they seemed to find their contours inviting.

Then Ola took her by the shoulders, and bent to dry her face with his sleeve. Cupping her face in his hands, he kissed her softly for the first time. He held her in the moonlight, and the two of them rocked together slowly back and forth looking at the moon on the water.

"There is a cabin near Laerdal that belongs to my brother's farm. It is where I would like you to stay with Henrik through the rest of the summer. It will be cozier for the two of you than the farmhouse at Lysne gärd. You would have your own house. And I will come visit while I am on leave."

She bent back to look up at him.

"After what you have told me about the risk to my reputation? No. You may visit, but not stay, Ola Lysne. If you want to marry, fine, perhaps we shall bed when I have my bowl and spoon and our betrothal is official and I turn nineteen or twenty. But I will not bed with you until then. That is my requirement." Randine had pushed him away by now and was looking straight into his moonlit face so he could see she was serious.

"Randine, we can night-court. No one will know." Ola tried to pry her loose from her stance. He reached for her again.

"Night-court, are you serious?" she said. "That is how I got pregnant the first time!"

"You city girl, night-courting is different in the country. Men come to visit at night, and the couple sleeps together for a few hours. Then he leaves again in the night, or he stays, and leaves before their chores in the morning," Ola reported.

"Yes, well I have heard of it, it seems the same as in the city. It is how James and I got together ...and created our son! But you have strange names for this custom in Laerdal." She said stifling a smiling and shaking her head.

"It is not just Laerdal, it happens all over though it has other names. It is a good way for shy couples to get to know each other, away from gossip. Sometimes they just talk for months, and sit by the fire before they bed."

She took her rock solid stance again, pushing away his hands, and crossing her arms under her breasts. "Ola Lysne, I will not allow you to night-court me. If you want to visit me, and your son during the evening hours, you may. Otherwise, you sleep in the barn, or sleep at your brother's house."

"But it is miles from the cabin, you cannot make me walk back to his farm!" Ola was angry now. He did not expect her to be so firm on this.

"No, you will not night-court this woman. We do not want gossip flying, and we do not want to start rumors! You said this yourself." Randine was firm.

"Now you sound like Ursula. Did she put you up to this?" Ola was teasing her, but he was serious too.

"Ursula has nothing to do with this. Until we marry, or are at least engaged, we will not sleep together, that is final. At least my virtue will not be questioned. They already know you're a sailor." Now she was teasing him.

"Randine, you are being unreasonable," Ola begged.

"Too bad, I think your town rules are unreasonable too. Especially when I have been told that half the young families in the country have parents that are not married for years. They come to the altar with several children in tow. Ursula told me. So much for your night-courting," she stated flatly.

"That is with cotters. Not with farmers, not with corporals or sergeants. It is different Randine." Ola was serious again. He did not like her stance on this issue.

"Ah, so there are two sets of rules, I see, one for the cotters and one for the farmers. And who are the farmers trying to impress, the preachers?" Randine was turning sarcastic, and Ola did not like it one bit.

"Stop, you are not being fair," Ola said.

"Fair, I don't think the young women have a fair shake in any regard. If I have to wait three or four years, you will too. That is fair." Randine turned back to the house and began walking away. Ola grabbed her arm and swung her around. He planted a kiss on her until she stopped struggling and she put her arms around his long neck.

"You must know I love you Randine, that is what I wanted to say. Believe me. There is no one else I would bring to home to Laerdal. I love you, and you have ruined it for me with anyone else," Ola said more deeply than he ever had.

Randine was startled by his confession. She did not expect this for some time. Suddenly she was flooded by his warmth and passion.

"I, I believe you, Ola." She kissed him this time, and they spent a long time touching each other's faces and then kissing again. When Randine felt she was ready to throw out her moral stance right then and there and make love to Ola she pulled away and placed her hand on his broad chest.

"But you will be the one to have to prove it with your actions, Ola Lysne. I have already by coming here with no other promise than to be with Henrik. We will both have to from the sound of it in this small valley. Now, good night, good rest, I have to check on Henrik."

Ola did not follow but watched Randine as she walk away. He would marry her someday. He was smiling now.

She was relieved that at last between the two of them, they spoke of it. She felt elated and sad at the same time. Two and half years before a wedding was too much! But thank God he would be gone for most of it. At least he would be out of temptation's reach. He would not be living with her, or would he? It would be more difficult for both of them, now that they had kissed and intentions to each other were a bit clearer. Yet, if they married now, even with their ages an issue, to wait for him always to come home from sea, with more babies to tend for sure, and alone raising them, she knew they were making the better choice.

Ola did not return to the ferryman's house right away. He stood by the water for a long time. With the enchanted moon and the mountains reflecting in the fjord, he felt back in his land now. Tomorrow he would be home. As if his thoughts were heard by the serpent Jormungand, a fish jumped, its tail flashing light then dark under a bright moon.

The End
and an uncertain
new beginning...

See Book Two
The Legend of Randine:
The Laerdal Letters

About the Author

Robin Heerens Lysne has always been interested in ancestral history, creativity, and cultural change. Born and raised in Rockford, Illinois, her writing reflects the landscapes of the Midwest, and her love of California where she has lived since 1987.

Robin is an author of seven books on topics of health, healing, poetry, and metaphysics. Currently she is launching an "Ancestral Women's Series," with two works of historical fiction to bring to life the courage and wisdom of her Norwegian ancestors. *The Legend of Randine: Entering the Sisterhood,* is her first novel. *The Legend of Randine: The Laerdal Letters,* the second novel in the novel series will be published in 2022, through Blue Bone Books.

Her earlier books center on energy medicine and metaphysical healing, tapping into heart centeredness and intuition. A natural entrepreneur, in 2006 she founded a cooperative publishing house, Blue Bone Books, which publishes poetry and works by a variety of Northern California authors including herself. Her latest release is *Unearthed*, a book of poems from the Emerald Street Poets.

Her education began as an art student in Milwaukee at the University of Wisconsin where she received her B.F.A. in painting and drawing. Moving to Michigan, she later became a curator at the Ella Sharp Museum, in Jackson, Michigan, and taught art through Michigan art centers and Art History at Jackson Community College, and was an exhibiting artists. As an artist she has shown widely from New York City to Santa Cruz, CA. Her artwork explores cultural and spiritual themes embedded in nature as well as abstractions inspired by human auras and energy healing.

Her interest in personal transformation extends into her work as a professional medium, psychic and energy medicine practitioner. In her 30 years experience she offers her clients safety, intuitive insight, compassion and mentoring.

In the late 1980's she made her way to California for advanced studies in cultural change, energy medicine and creative writing. She earned her first Masters in Spirituality and Psychology (Holy Names University), an M.F.A. in Creative Writing (Mills College) and a Ph.D. in Energy Medicine, (University of Natural Medicine).

Based in Santa Cruz, CA, she attracts a global audience and gives lectures and workshops as an author, meditation teacher, intuitive/medium, mentor and coach. Her websites are:

www.thecenterforthesoul.com
www.bluebonebooks.com
www.RobinLysne.com.

Acknowledgements

There are many people to thank for getting the story of Randine to you, the reader. The first are all the editors and friends who helped in the shaping of *Randine*.

Maggie Paul, a long time sister-friend, and fellow poet, went over the first drafts of this manuscript years ago. She helped me shape the story and hone the writing a great deal. Nelda Warren was another friend who helped a me, especially discerning if this was a story for me to tell. Mills College professors Ruth Saxton, and Patricia Powell taught me more than I can say about prose writing, especially Patricia Powell, who supported the story, and helped me get unstuck with certain points in the Randine's story. Both teachers were exceptional in their help. Kendra Langeteig was the final draft editor who was so helpful in her feedback and support in fine tuning the story and understanding Norwegian culture.

In Norway, various government agencies, including the Midwifery school in Oslo were very helpful in confirming Randine's attendance and graduation from the Midwifery school in the early days, which shaped the second volume and it's location, etc. The University of Bergen, in Bergen Norway along with the Laerdal Tourist Bureau, which introduced me to the Big Book, and helped me to understand some of the records kept by the government on emigration, including birth and death dates, as well as Randine's graduation from the early midwifery school.

I also appreciate the support from friends and family that made *Randine* what it is today. My two nieces, Lysne Tait and Laura Knudson, were both very helpful and gave feedback about differences in births. Since 1995 with my trip to Laerdal, I especially want to thank my distant cousin, Hoken Lysne, who gave me a great tour of the family farm and original house in Laerdal. It was time well spent that I will never forget, including he and his wife's hospitality.

My sister and brother-in-law Nancy and Ralph who read the screenplay and gave great feedback. I also want to give a huge thanks to my midwives, Kate Bowman and the late Roxanne Cummings, who inspired me to write about midwifery with their amazing service and wisdom to me.

I also want to thank the spirit of Randine, who gave me permission to write this book, and who lives through all of my sisters, nieces, and cousins, who are already strong, self-determined women in their own right, who I hope will be even more inspired by Randine's example unto the seventh generation.

Books by the Author

Ancestral Women's Series
Book One: The Legend of Randine:
Entering the Sisterhood

Book Two: The Legend of Randine:
The Laerdal Letters (2022)

Ceremonies from the Heart
for Children, Adults and the Earth

Mosaic, New and Collected Poems

Poems for the Lost Deer

Heart Path Handbook, For Therapists
and Healers

Heart Path Learning to love Yourself
and Listening to Your Guides

all by Blue Bone Books, Santa Cruz, CA,

Living a Sacred Life

Dancing Up the Moon,
A Woman's Guide to Creating Traditions
that Bring Sacredness to Daily Life,

published by Conari Press, Berkeley, CA.

OTHER BOOKS BY:

Blue Bone Books

Summer Street
        by Margaret Bond Smith

Path of the Heart CD
        by the author

You Long for Me
        by Amita

Understory
        by Marcia Adams

Infared
                by Janet Trenchard

Visible Light
        by Stuart Presley

Heart Calls, Soul Answers
        by Biraj Palmer

Unearthed
        by the Emeralds Street Poets

CPSIA information can be obtained
at www.ICGtesting.com
Printed in the USA
FSHW012239181121
86330FS